The Narrow Gate

By Christine Stearns

1

This is a work of fiction. Names, characters, places, and incidents are the product of the author's imagination. Any resemblance to actual persons, living or dead, businesses, locations, or events is entirely coincidental. Thank you.

Dedication

This book is dedicated to my beautiful grandson, Brett Michael Salamin Jr., who died this year in a terrible accident. Our whole family mourns him every day. He lived his life with great joy and energy. He taught us all to appreciate every moment. He loved us with his great heart. Brett Michael, I love you "so much in the whole world." As you would say.

The book is also dedicated to my Mom and Dad, my niece Sarah Richardson Burns, and my nephew Seamus Rustin—angels who have gone before us. They have taught me so much about life and love. I am eternally grateful, and I hope and pray that they will be waiting for me when I cross the finish line. When I can say, as St. Paul says, "I have fought the good fight. I have finished the race. I have kept the faith."

Acknowledgments

I could not have written this book without the endless support and encouragement of my husband, Christopher Stearns. He was my first reader and editor. Furthermore, I want to thank my children, who also reviewed the manuscript and offered ideas and suggestions. Finally, I must thank my grandchildren, who gave me advice about dialogue. Invaluable advice, as I tried to get it right. Beyond that, I must thank my sisters and brothers and my extended family, many of whom also acted as early readers of the story. Finally, thank you to my wonderful friends, who always believed in me and encouraged me in my writing.

Chapter One

The winds of autumn rustled in the poplar trees, and the fat, yellow leaves let go of their slender branches and gave up their spirits. The sun slanted sharply through the branches, now opening spaces more and more every day. Annie strolled out into her backyard and sat on the warm September grassy lawn. She looked up at the poplar trees, and watched the leaves whirling down. The poplars were her most and her least favorite trees. Most favorite because they got their leaves so early in the spring. Least favorite because they gave up the ghost so easily. They just couldn't seem to muster enough fight to hang on. The oak trees at the far corner of the yard were much braver. They turned red and yellow before they turned brown, and they might easily keep their leaves until Thanksgiving Day. Soon after that, they gave up too, but they fought a lot more courageously than the stupid old poplar trees.

In spite of their cowardice, however, Annie had to admit a grudging kind of admiration for the poplars. First of all, they did make their presence felt very early in the season—starting to leaf out in late April or early May. Eager to embrace the first warm days, they drunkenly pushed out their leaves. She had to admire that. Secondly, there was the thing about the leaves

themselves. They were heart shaped.
Really and truly heart shaped. Thirdly, they
had great big leaves that sounded a little bit
like someone politely clapping their hands.
So, in spite of their autumnal weaknesses,
she had to admit a fondness for them.

Her mom had died two years ago, on
this very day. September 3. Annie
remembered standing in the cemetery after
the funeral Mass. Standing with the rest of
her family, all dressed in black, quietly
crying as her mother's casket was lowered
into the ground. The cemetery was full of
poplar trees. They had tumbled their yellow
leaves down on them as the minister said a
final prayer. She had been twelve years old.
Now, she was almost fifteen, and she had so
many questions she would have like to ask
her mom. Her dad was doing the best job he
could with everything, but he was not her
mom. Not even close.

Annie looked up at the afternoon
sky. It was a brilliant blue. You could
almost believe it was still summer, looking
at the sky. Almost, but not quite. If you
closed your eyes and sniffed the air, you
could smell the fall. A faint but persistent
smell of things decaying. Of leaves falling.
Of school starting. Annie opened her eyes
and looked at the old poplar trees. A big,
fat, yellow leaf tumbled toward her and hit
her right on the heart. Annie picked it up off
the grass where it had eventually fallen. She

went inside the house and put the leaf in her favorite book. A collection of Winnie the Pooh stories she had been given on her seventh birthday by her mom. The one where her mom had written inside: "To Annie. May this book give you pleasure every time you pick it up. Now and always. Happy birthday. Love, Mom." Annie placed the yellow leaf right inside the book and put the book back on her bookshelf.

Annie had been a big deal in middle school. By the end of the eighth grade, she knew everybody in the school, and everybody in the school knew her story. But St. Patrick's was a small school, and Central High was an entirely different entity. A different solar system. Still, in two days, she would walk through those front doors and begin her life there.

She liked to think about beginnings because she had had enough of endings. The whole idea of a fresh beginning had some real appeal—if she could just keep from screwing things up. However, some things were not about to change, not any time soon anyhow. Her brother and sister were still little, in third and fourth grade at St. Pat's. She would still have to pick them up at the end of the school day, at least sometimes, and walk home with them. And get dinner going for the family before her dad got home. Her dad taught science at the high school. But, he only taught seniors, AP physics. She wouldn't have him for a teacher for at least three years. And only if she did well in her earlier science classes. So, for a while, she was safe. Maybe people wouldn't even put two and two together, realizing that he was her dad. Maybe for a while she could stay anonymous. That seemed like the best plan. Let him have his life there, and she would try to have her own. But, it was going to get a lot busier in just two days. She would have to get up and go to school, and get her brother and sister ready for their school day. Plus homework, plus helping Eddie and Sarah with theirs. Plus laundry. And then cooking dinner.

But still—during the day at Central, she might be able to invent a whole new identity for herself. She could finally ditch the uniform. She would wear Jeans and a t-shirt. And tennis shoes. It sounded like heaven after wearing a school uniform for eight years. She ran upstairs, listening to the kids playing in the family room. The whole house was open today. A warm September breeze was blowing through the open windows. Dad was in the family room watching football, of course, with her brother and sister at his feet. Eddie was half watching football with Dad, and half playing some new free video game on his Ipad. Sarah was cutting up paper hearts to glue on another big sheet of paper. She was painstakingly writing "I love u" on each of the hearts. The misspelling of "you" sort of bugged Annie, and she wanted to correct her, but she decided to use the peace and quiet to her advantage and slip upstairs to her room. Time to go through her clothes and plan the week.

Tomorrow was Labor Day, the unofficial last day of summer, and everything started up for real the next day. Her dad had tomorrow off, so he had a three-day weekend. But Annie felt all jittery. There would be so many new people. Would she be able to find her classrooms? Would she make friends? Would any guy even look at her? The whole thing was terrifying. She went in her room and flopped on her bed. Right next to her bed was her dresser with her most important pictures framed. The most important one of all was the one of her and her mom.

The picture had been taken on one of the last good days. Her mom was already getting way too thin, and her hair was starting to fall out from the chemo. But, as Annie held the picture in her hands and looked at it, she thought that her mom was the most beautiful woman in the world. She had this sad but intense light in her eyes, as if she saw everything—the past, the present, and the future. She had been dead for two years now, but it seemed like yesterday that she had sat by her mother's side, holding her hand. When the last day came, Annie brought a photo album to show her mom as they spent those last precious hours together. She sat by her side, climbing right up on the hospital bed, turning the pages so that the last thing her mom saw in this world would be their loving faces, smiling at her. Her mom had drifted in and out of a morphine haze. The morphine was the only thing that could dull the pain at the end. But, as Annie turned the pages, her mom had tried to focus on the pictures. Annie heard her whisper, "Beautiful. Beautiful. Beautiful." In fact, that was the last word that Annie had ever heard her mom say. Beautiful. It still amazed her that her mom could say that even as she was suffering so much, even as she was dying. But, because it was the last thing she heard her mom say, the word had a kind of magical quality to it. Magical, or sacred. Something like that.

Since then, Annie had moved from counting days to counting months. In the beginning, she used to say to herself every night, "It's been thirteen days since Mom died." At some point, she went over this invisible line—she didn't even know where it was exactly—where she switched to months. Now, it had been twenty-four months, two years, since her mom left her. But it didn't seem like the ache was getting any better. Everyone said, "Give it time." She wondered what they meant by "time."

Did they mean days? Or months? Or years? Time did not seem to be helping very much. Not yet anyway.

She put the picture back on the dresser and lay still on her bed, listening to the last of the summer winds rustle the leaves on the old poplar tree. Ever since she was a baby, it was one of her favorite sounds. It sounded like the leaves on the tree were softly clapping their hands. Or like the whisper of angels' wings. Or something very special. Momma used to park her baby buggy under the poplar tree and let her take her nap right out there in the yard in the summer. Her mom had told her the story hundreds of times. The other night, hungering for further validation, she asked her dad about the baby buggy. He just sadly smiled and said, "I really don't remember, Annie, but if your mom told you that story, then it must be true."

Somehow, it hurt Annie's feelings that he handled it that way. It kind of felt like maybe it was just a nice story, and not true at all. However, as she lay on her bed right now, listening to the leaves tapping each other, she could not believe that her mom would make something like that up. She closed her eyes and tried to recall how her mom smelled. She had an old scarf of her mom's in her top drawer. She reached in there and pulled it out, and reclosing her eyes, sniffed the scarf. It seemed to be losing its scent. It was purple and blue, like a bruised twilight sky. Her mom's favorite colors. She held it to her face and tried to conjure up her mom, tried to will herself into a dream where she would be there.

Instead, Sarah came quietly into the room and crawled up on the bed with her. "Annie," she said. "Are you trying to find momma again? Can I come with you?" Annie realized, once again, how little Sarah was.

Annie opened her eyes and reached for her little sister. "No. Really, I was just listening to the music of the old poplar tree. I love the sound the leaves make when they slap against each other. Lie still here and listen. Hear it?"

Sarah snuggled into her armpit. Her blond hair, like corn silk, tickled Annie's face, but Annie just let it be. She said, "You know, Sarah. When you were a baby, momma used to park your buggy right out there under the poplar tree. And let you take your afternoon nap right out there. You loved the sound of the leaves. You went right to sleep, just like a baby." Sarah smiled as Annie told her this story. Annie didn't really know if it was true, but it was such a great story that she wanted to give it to her sister. She knew that her mom had told her that she used to do that for her, so it stood to reason that she did it for Sarah too. Annie was beginning to realize that stories and memories intertwine and become your past. She was just starting to figure that out, and she realized further that stories had a kind of power, all their own. She listened to Sarah's gentle, slow breathing and tried to match her breaths to her sister's. In and out. In and out. Just breathe. Just breathe. Just breathe.

The last days of summer. The school year was upon them, and Annie didn't know what to expect of this whole new school. Her mind drifted to the sounds coming in from the window. Somewhere in the distance, somebody was mowing the lawn. The sound of laughter drifted in from the backyard of the house next door. It sounded like the neighbors were having a barbecue, and the kids were splashing in the pool. It was probably the last swim of the summer. Annie was filled with a soft sadness, listening to the leaves, listening to her sister's gentle breathing, thinking about her mom, wondering what the school year held, and feeling the last warm breeze coming in the window. Without meaning to, she closed her eyes.

Chapter 2

Suddenly, it was all too real. Her dad had
dropped her brother and sister off at St.
Patrick's. There were all kinds of moms
there helping out on the first day, and almost
everybody knew Sarah and Eddie. Lots of
people called out a hello to them as they
trudged up the big stone steps, bent over
from the weight of their new backpacks,
filled with their new school supplies. Annie
had helped her dad work through their list of
"mandatory" school supplies. Annie knew
that there was no way they needed all that
stuff in their cubby on the first day, but there
was no way either Eddie or Sarah would
believe that. They wanted everything on the
list, packed away in their cubby, with their
names on it. Annie remembered how
conscientiously her mom had done all that
for her, so she tried to help her dad get it
right for the kids. They made their way up
the steps, and Eddie went right in. He didn't
turn around and wave. Maybe that was a
good sign, Annie thought. One of his best
buddies was waiting for him on the top step.
But Sarah turned around and waved to them
before she went in. Annie was glad that her
dad had waited for a minute so that they
were there to wave back. He put the car and
drive and pulled forward in the car line.
Traffic was all backed up with all the moms
and dads dropping their children off. But

they finally got out of the parking lot, and he drove to Central High. "Do you know where your homeroom is, Annie?" he asked. "Do you need me to walk you there?"

Annie cringed. "Don't worry. I've got my whole day mapped out. But thanks anyhow. I have a secret little map taped in the back of one of my notebooks. So I can consult it if I get turned around."

Her dad smiled. "I knew I didn't have to worry about you. I knew you would figure it all out. Do you need lunch money?" he asked.

She rolled her eyes, trying to keep it together. "Nope," she said. "I decided to brown bag it today because I didn't want to have to wait in line. I just want to find a quiet corner and collect my wits when lunch time comes."

He parked the car in his faculty spot, grabbed his briefcase, and gave her a quick kiss on the cheek. Suddenly, Annie had a thought that her dad seemed a little nervous today too. Maybe first days are rough on everybody, although her dad had been doing this for a long time now. Still, it kind of made her feel not quite so bad about her own nervousness. She had eaten a bowl of cereal this morning, but her stomach was making weird noises just the same. Like she had forgotten to eat. Butterflies, her mom used to call them. A cute name for something not so cute.

"See you after school," her dad said. "Room 201."

"Got it," she said, leaping out of the car and heading for her homeroom. Room 109. Way at the other end of the school. There were hundreds of teenagers milling around everywhere. Annie felt a lump in her throat. She swallowed hard and dove into the mess of students.

Chapter 3

Right away Annie knew that she was going
to like Mrs. Murphy. As the students filed
into the room, Mrs. Murphy said, "Good
morning. You can sit anywhere you want
today. I will make a seating chart based on
where you want to sit. Make yourselves
comfortable." She said the same thing to
everyone that came in. Annie had never
heard anything like that before. At St. Pat's
the seating charts were always alphabetical.
So, as Annie Simmons, she usually showed
up near the end of the list, and she usually
got assigned a seat in the back of the room.
Which was fine. But, she thought to herself,
since I get a choice, why not mix it up. So,
she counted two desks over from the front
door, and three desks back. For two parents
and three kids. Also for her birthday,
February third. She realized, even as she did
it, that it was a pretty silly way to pick a
desk, but it seemed like as good a way as
any other. Annie sat down and looked
around the room. Mrs. Murphy was her
homeroom teacher and she was also going to
be her teacher for Freshman Honors English.
Annie was a really good test taker, and she
always had good grades, so she had all
honors classes. She was a little nervous
about this, but her dad insisted that she
should take the hardest classes she could.
That she should challenge herself. And he

knew all the teachers on staff and had assured her that she would like all her teachers. She had decided to reserve judgment on that, but she had to admit that she had a good feeling about Mrs. Murphy.

As Annie looked around the room, she could see that Mrs. Murphy had a lot of artwork up for what must be the first thing they were going to read together—*The Scarlet Letter*. The artwork showed a beautiful young mom holding a baby in her arms. And she had a big red "A" stitched on her dress. The mom looked proud and aloof, and in the distance, there was a creepy, bent over old man looking at her with what might be hatred in his eyes. Annie wondered if he intended to do harm to the pretty young mother. Or her baby.

All around her, other kids were filing in to the classroom. Mrs. Murphy continued to greet them, and Annie saw the surprised look on their faces when she told them that they could sit anywhere they want to. Some of them looked puzzled; others looked wary. Some came in very quietly, like she had done. But some of them strutted in like they owned the place. One guy—a kid named Dylan who was very hot, and who knew it— was wearing a shirt with the Budweiser logo on it. He swaggered into the room, throwing his book bag on the floor by the lockers, grinning confidently. Mrs. Murphy stopped him right at the door and shook her head.

"Dean's office. Now. Come back when you're wearing something school appropriate."

"But," he sputtered.

"No buts," Mrs. Murphy answered firmly. "Go change what you have on."

Annie looked at her with a new level of respect. She might seem kind, but underneath, there was something very strong. She was not the least bit impressed by Dylan's bravado, and she sent him packing. Almost every other kid in the room watched the whole encounter with veiled interest. Most of the kids had their cell phones out and were rapidly typing away, thumbs flying as texts recorded the whole incident. Suddenly, the homeroom bell rang. Mrs. Murphy moved to the front of the class and called the class to attention.

"Good morning, ladies and gentlemen," she said. Annie heard someone snicker softly in the back of the room. Mrs. Murphy went on as if she had not heard it, but Annie was willing to bet that she had. "Put your cell phones away. Right now. Turn them to silent or turn them off. Do not put them in your pockets. Put them in your book bags, and put those bags under your desk. If I see any of you using a cell phone, I will confiscate it for the day. You may have it back at the end of the school day, but not until them. All right? Does everyone understand? Very good. When I call your name, please answer 'present.' Let me hear you speak plainly. I will look up and see your face. I am also going to make a seating chart. Not today, because you don't know exactly where you would like to sit. But tomorrow. So, look around the room during the course of the hour today and figure out where you want to sit. Then, sit there tomorrow and we will make our chart. You may sit where you have chosen to sit unless you prove yourself unworthy of that choice. Understood? Yes? Good." She then proceeded to call the role. Annie had never seen anything like it. Most of the other students seemed to be a little stunned too. This Mrs. Murphy might be pretty, might seem kind, but there was some kind of steel underneath that sweet exterior. Annie decided that she liked what she saw.

Mrs. Murphy finished with the attendance and then said, "Now, all of you are in my homeroom, and we will begin each day together. You have the locker right here in the room. I am also your first period teacher. Each one of you is enrolled in Freshman Honors English class. So. We go right from homeroom into English. The homeroom period is fifteen minutes. You may use the time as you see fit. But you may not use your cell phone at any time in this room. Now, I will assign your lockers and you will have a couple minutes to see if you can figure out the lock. Help each other. Keep it quiet. When I call your name, come up to me and get your locker number and your combination. We will finish all of this by 8:15. Then, we will begin our first period English class together." Mrs. Murphy gave them precisely five minutes to find their lockers and get back to their seats, ready for English class.

Annie was impressed by how organized she was. When she was called up, she got her locker and her combination. She tried it out and it worked right away. She knew what to do because her dad had been over all of this with her. So, she opened her locker and put her book bag in there, along with her cell phone. She could see other kids struggling to work the combinations.

One girl was struggling with her combination, getting more and more frustrated. Annie said, "Can I help you with that?"

The girl, who was very slender and very blond, looked at Annie gratefully. "I would really appreciate it. I don't know what I'm doing wrong, but I can't get it. And now my fingers are so nervous that I can hardly twirl the stupid dial." Two bright red spots had appeared on the girl's cheeks.

Annie laughed and said, "Well, hello. My name is Annie. Let me see if I can help."

"Oh, man," the girl said. "Where are my manners? My name's Olivia. But you can call me Livvie if you like. Or Olivia. Either one is fine. I just moved here and I don't know anybody. And I don't know how to do this either. I suck."

Annie took the lock in her hands and twirled the top dial to the right several times. She said, "The trick is to kind of clear everything out by twirling it to the right for a few times. I usually do it three times because there are three kids in my family. Then, slow down and do the first number. Then, go the other way past the first number to the second number. Then go the first way to the third number." The lock clicked open in her hands. "Here," she said. "You try it."

Olivia talked herself through the process, and the lock clicked open for her too. She grinned at Annie. "Thanks a lot. That is the first good thing that has happened today."

Annie smiled. "Well, let's hope it's not the last." They finished as the bell rang and took their seats. Annie noticed that Olivia had chosen a desk right beside hers, quite by accident. Olivia smiled at Annie and they both sat down.

Chapter 4

As the bell rang to begin first hour class, Mrs. Murphy stood up at the front of the class. There was something about her that made the class quiet down quickly. A couple of kids in the back of the class slumped in their seats and made a big show of talking a little bit longer than they were supposed to, but Mrs. Murphy just ignored them, seeming somehow to recognize their behavior as very immature and therefore unworthy of her attention. They got quiet pretty quickly. She smiled, "Good morning, everybody. Today we begin our study of freshman honor's English together. Since you are an honor's class, I will assume that you have already mastered the basic principles of grammar and I will not bore you with a repetition of those rules. I will address grammar as problems arise in your writing—that is to say—when I notice that you are having a problem with some grammar rule, I will talk about it. Otherwise, we will be turning our focus to some of the great writers and thinkers who have gone before us. And we will start today with Nathaniel Hawthorne's famous novel entitled *The Scarlet Letter*. You were told to bring a copy of it to class today. Please get your copy out. Also, try to have a pen and a highlighter. No electronic devices are allowed. We are old school here."

Many of the students started rearranging things on their desks, finding their copy of the book. Several of them whined that they didn't know that they would have to have the book on the first day, that they hadn't expected to have to do work on the first day. Mrs. Murphy smiled gently and told them that they would be working every day, that they had been told to bring a paperback copy of the book, and that they had better get out a sheet of paper and prepare to take notes. Again, Annie heard that quiet steel in her voice. The kids searched for paper and got ready to take notes.

Mrs. Murphy said, "This novel opens with a prologue that nobody likes to read very much. In fact, a lot of very bright students have told me that they read it carefully, and that they never really figured out why it matters. In fact, it almost turned them off to the whole book. And that would be a very sad thing because it is really a wonderful story. So, let me tell you what matters in this first chapter, and then we will move on. You see, in this prologue, *The Custom House*, Hawthorne introduces his narrator. He tells the reader that he worked in a custom house, and that in the course of his working there, he found a bunch of old documents and a faded, but still very beautiful scarlet letter. About three and a half inches tall, made of beautiful scarlet material and embroidered with gold thread.

Somehow, he couldn't get it out of his mind, and he read the documents and then pieced the story together, of a beautiful young woman who had borne a child out of wedlock. And was forced to wear the letter on the bodice of her clothing every day. And the letter 'A' branded her as an adultress, an outcast, someone who is not fit to live in polite society."

A hand went up in the back of the room. "Excuse me, Mrs. Murphy," the student said. He was a quiet young man with dark hair. Annie did not know his name. "What does that word mean exactly?"

Mrs. Murphy answered very plainly, "First of all, let me get your name. Brendon? All right. Thank you. Well, to answer your question—it means that she had a baby, and that she was not married. That she must have had an affair with some man, a man who was not her husband. For this, she is shamed, and many people think that the baby should be taken from her, and that she should be hanged as punishment for her sin."

Another hand went up in the back of the room. A girl this time. She said that her name was Gabriella, and then she said, "But Mrs. Murphy. People do that all the time. I mean, have sex without being married. And have babies without being married. How can it be that it was such a big deal back then?" Annie wasn't sure if the girl was trying to be cool, or if she was genuinely puzzled. She decided to give her the benefit of the doubt.

Apparently, Mrs. Murphy did too. She smiled gently and said, "Well, you're right. People do have sex without being married. And in our time, watching television and movies, you might think that there are no consequences for young people today. But, I think you had better be careful about that kind of thinking. Maybe we don't make young women wear scarlet letters on the bosom of their gowns, but we often brand them in quieter ways. Quieter, but perhaps just as painful. You think about that. And let us take a look at chapter one together." Everybody that had a book turned to chapter one. Those that didn't have books were frantically scribbling. Annie was willing to be that they would have their books by tomorrow.

Mrs. Murphy said, "Now the first chapter is called 'The Prison Door.' Read it along with me while I read it to you." She began to read the chapter, in a really beautiful reading voice, and Annie sat there and felt the magic of the words steal over her. When Mrs. Murphy came to the end of the chapter, which was a very short one, there was this passage about a beautiful wild rose outside the ugly prison door. Annie immediately knew in her heart that this rose

was a symbol. And that was exactly what
Mrs. Murphy said. She asked them to think
about it, and to read the next chapter for
homework tonight. And to see if they could
figure out the symbolism and be ready to
talk about it. Annie felt a deep excitement
in her heart. The whole class was actually
buzzing with a quiet excitement as the bell
rang.

Chapter 5

Annie went by her dad's classroom at the end of the school day, and there were lots of kids in there talking to her dad. He knew a lot of them from the year before. He had taught some of them chemistry as juniors, and now, as seniors, they were in his AP Physics class. She could see that he was happy to be reunited with them. He was smiling and laughing. Since her mom had died, she had not seen him laugh all that often, so it was good to see him enjoying himself.

"How about I just walk home," Annie said to her dad. "Just come when you're ready. Mrs. Allen is bringing the munchkins home today, isn't she?"

Her dad smiled at her. "You sure? You all right with that? Got your house key?" He had his worry lines on his forehead.

Annie smiled back. "Yeah. I got it. It's fine. Take your time. I want to walk a while after being cooped up all day. But I had a good day. A really good day." She added this quickly, knowing that he would want to hear that.

"Okay," he said. "Be careful. I'll be home soon. You got your cell phone?"

Annie grinned at him and held her cell phone up so he could see it. He seemed to worry more about her, about everything, since her mom had died.

Then, she noticed that he almost seemed grateful as he turned his attention back to his adoring flock. She smiled and waved goodbye to him and headed out to the parking lot. As she walked through the parking lot, she saw lots of the older students climbing into their cars, racing out of the lot. In the distance, she noticed Olivia climbing into a big Mercedes. Olivia caught her eye and waved. Annie waved back, and headed through the lot to the sidewalk that ran along the road. Soon, she had left the noise of the school behind.

She felt the warm, late summer breeze on her skin. She felt the wind lift her hair. It all felt good. She sometimes told herself that when she felt these gentle touches from the natural world, it was really her mom reaching out from the next world, telling her that she loved her. Annie knew that it was just her imagination, but it was such a powerful image that she was loath to shake it off. She walked along the road and came to the cut off that she liked to take. There were old train tracks that were no longer used. The city had turned them into a jogging and biking trail. They were not really ever very busy, and Annie had come to think of it as her secret place. There was a huge old oak tree that shaded the entrance to the tracks, and a narrow gate that you had to pass through to enter the trail. Sometimes, Annie liked to sit there, just for a little while, to let her mind drift on the quiet, with no one else around to see her or bother her.

She approached the gate, where the earth was covered with a gentle, grassy moss, and sat down, with her back against the gate. She set her book bag down and leaned back, feeling the coolness of the shade and the late summer breeze. She noticed that there was a wild rose growing by the side of the gate. She remembered the wild rose outside the prison door in *The Scarlet Letter*. This rose bush was covered with red blooms, bees buzzing frantically around it, trying to get the last bit of sweetness before summer disappeared again. She sat there watching the bees in their feverish activity, and suddenly the smell of the roses drifted to her on the breeze. She closed her eyes, leaning against the gate, and let the quiet pleasure of the moment take her away. In her mind, she remembered a song her mom used to sing to her long ago. It was by the poet Robert Burns. "My Luve is like a red, red rose." Her mom had the softest voice. She used to sing the song to her at bedtime. Annie had memorized the words long ago, without ever really trying to. The words were just there in her head. It seemed as though they always had been.

O, my luve's like a red, red rose
That's newly sprung in June.
O, my luve is like a melodie
That's sweetly played in tune.
As fair art thou, my bonnie lass,
So deep in luve am I;
And I will luve thee still, my dear,
Till all the seas gang dry.
Till all the seas gang dry, my dear,
And the rocks melt with the sun.
And I will luve thee still, my dear,
While the sands of life shall run.
So, fare thee weel, my only luve,
And fare thee weel a while.
And I will come again, my luve,
Though it were ten thousand mile.

She kept her eyes closed and listened to the voice in her head. Singing the sweet words of that song. When she was a little girl, it used to seem like just a love song. But now that she was older, she heard the undercurrent of sadness in the song. The person who was singing the song was saying goodbye. He had to go away, and he didn't want to. Or she had to go away. And she hoped that she could come back; she wanted to come back. If it were within her power, she would come back. But she would never, never stop loving the person she was singing to. Never stop loving. Annie kept her eyes closed tight, trying to hold her mom's voice in her head. She reached up and dried a tear that was working its way down her cheek. This would not do, she said to herself. This would not do at all. She opened her eyes and the first thing she saw was the wild rose bush, growing beside the gate. Carefully, watching out for the busy bees, she plucked a blossom and held it to her nose, leaning once more back on the gate. She closed her eyes and was suddenly aware of a strange feeling. A quiet buzzing or humming. Was it her mom's voice, starting the song again, coming from deep in her memory? Or was it the bees and their humming? She opened her eyes quickly and dropped the rose. The buzzing seemed to stop. All she could hear now was the gentle birdsong all around her, and the wind in the poplars. The sun was sinking lower in the sky. Time to go home. She got up slowly, looking at the gate. Looking at the rose lying on the moss. She shook off her reverie, picked up her book bag and started home. She must be tired out from the stress of the first day.

Chapter 6

The next day Dylan was back, with a plain black T-shirt on. And Jeans. But neat and clean. Annie watched him walk in out of the corner of her eye, never actually raising her eyes to look at him. He grinned at Mrs. Murphy and said, "Good morning, ma'am." Annie wasn't sure if there was a kind of taunting voice underneath his words, but she decided to give him the benefit of the doubt since Mrs. Murphy seemed indifferent to his tone. The homeroom period passed quickly, and Olivia was able to open her own locker. She quietly smiled at Annie, as if thanking her for the locker lesson yesterday.

Then English class began. Mrs. Murphy said that she wanted to talk about the second chapter today, the one entitled "The Market Place," where Hester is made to stand in front of everyone in the town on the scaffold, holding her newborn baby in her arms. There was some discussion about how horrible it must have been for her, when Dylan raised his hand. He said, "Do you mean to tell me that she had to wear this big red A on her chest, and all the men were looking at her tits for three hours." Annie felt the whole class kind of hold its breath, because Dylan had clearly tried to shock Mrs. Murphy with his language.

Annie felt her own cheeks turn red, and a blush spreading over her own neck and chest. Mrs. Murphy seemed to count to ten or something. She didn't say a word for a minute or two. The silence hung in the classroom like a fog. A couple of Dylan's buddies started to giggle in the back of the room. Dylan kept looking at Mrs. Murphy, a slight smile on his lips. Mrs. Murphy looked down at the seating chart and said, "All right, Dylan. That's your name, right? It will take me a few days to learn all of your names, but I think I know yours already. Let me answer your question very carefully. First of all, we scholars don't use the word 'tits'. It is just not done by scholarly and intelligent people when talking about literature. However, having said that, let me acknowledge that you have actually brought us to a very astute observation." The class stirred, and the giggling stopped. "Get out your pens and highlighters and let's look at the end of the chapter, to the passage Dylan has referred to. He is actually absolutely right. There is a creepy kind of voyeurism at play here. All the good men and women of the town are staring at Hester's breasts. Hawthorne has told us that she is very tall and has an ample figure, and right now she is nursing a newborn baby, so we could be right in assuming that her breasts are rather noticeable. And every single person in that town spends three hours staring at her, men and women alike. Notice the comments made by many of the old women. They want to brand her with an A on her forehead, or hang her right there on the spot."

Olivia raised her hand. She said, very quietly, "I saw that there was one young woman who spoke kindly of Hester." She pointed out the passage. "But she was the only one who was nice at all." Mrs. Murphy agreed with her, and the discussion moved on. Annie tried to sneak a glance at Dylan to see how he seemed to be handling this moment. It seemed to Annie that Mrs. Murphy had kind of upstaged him very quietly, but she wasn't really sure how she had done it. She then moved the class on to a discussion of chapter three—the one where Reverend Dimmesdale tries to get Hester to publicly confess the name of her child's father. He makes an impassioned plea that she should tell her secret, and Hester replies, "I will not speak!" Mrs. Murphy was reading this part to the class, and Annie had the weird impression that Dimmesdale was actually relieved when she would not tell whose child it was.

Dylan raised his hand and said, "I think he's the dad."

A collective gasp went up from the class. Mrs. Murphy looked at Dylan and said, "Why do you think that?" Dylan did not seem at all unwilling to speak.

He said, "I just do. He sounds like he is really relieved that she won't talk. I

35

mean really relieved. That makes me wonder if he's got a reason to care that much." Mrs. Murphy actually kind of smiled at him. He dropped his eyes back to his book.

She said, "Interesting. We will let Dylan's theory just kind of float in the back of our minds for a while, and in the meantime, let me draw your attention to the shadowy figure standing at the back of the crowd, a man we will come to know as Roger Chillingworth. As you read the next two chapters tonight, I would like you to pay attention to this character. He will be a very important presence in the novel. There are only seven minutes left in the hour, so you may use that little bit of time to get started on your reading assignment for the night." Annie started to read the next chapter, but she tried to sneak a glance in at Dylan to see what he was up too. She could see that he had slipped his phone out of his pocket and was texting somebody, looking down at his book or seeming to. Annie was annoyed with him for being so predictably disrespectful, even in this sneaky way. Her eyes went back to the story, and soon the bell rang, sending her to Geometry. The best part of the day was over.

At the end of the school day, she went by her father's classroom. Once again, he was surrounded by his adoring throngs. He smiled at her and waved her over. She came to his desk and he said, "Hey, everybody. This is my daughter Annie. She is a freshman here this year." She felt herself get all red all over again, clutching her books tightly to her chest. These kids were all seniors in AP Physics, way out of her league. She felt their eyes on her, and they were all smiling. But she couldn't quite shake the impression that they were all looking at her as if she were some cute little puppy.

She said, "Hi, everybody. Nice to meet you." Although she did not remember a single one of their names. She turned to her dad. "Do you want me to swing by the school and pick up Sarah and Eddie. Or are you ready to go now, and we can pick them up together?"

He said, "Well, if you're really sure you don't mind, that would be great."

Annie was tired and was hoping that he would give her a ride home, but she smiled and said, "No problem. I will swing by and get them."

Her dad gave her a quick hug and said, "That would be a huge help to me, Annie. I have a big lab here tomorrow, and I could use another hour here to set it up. See if you can get them started on their homework if they have any." She nodded and said good-bye and headed out to the parking lot. She saw Olivia getting into the big, black Mercedes again and wondered what it would even feel like to ride around in a car like that. She saw Dylan hop on a small scooter, something like a Vespa, buckle a helmet on, and roar out of the parking lot. She wondered how that could even be. He had to be fourteen years old, like her, if he was in ninth grade honors English. Can you legally drive a scooter if you're fourteen? He roared right by her, with a black leather jacket on, and a black helmet. He never even looked her way. Par for the course, she thought. Why would he?

She started walking home and cut through the field next to the school. She came to the narrow gate that guarded the old train track and saw the wild rose bush guarding the gate. There were wild roses all over the town, which is why the town was called Old Rosedale, she guessed. Anyhow, there was no one around, and the kids' school did not get out for another forty minutes or so. So, she sat down by the narrow gate, letting the fragrance of the late summer roses waft over her. The sun was already setting in the west, and the angle of the sun caught her face and chest and warmed her. She spread her jacket on the grass so she had a comfy place to sit, leaned back on the gate and closed her eyes. Just for a minute. Or just for a couple minutes. The kids' school was only about a seven-minute walk from here, so a couple minutes would be fine. She surrendered. And

38

suddenly, she became aware of a strange humming in the back of her brain. Not an unpleasant one. What was that sound? Was she dreaming of her mom's voice again?

She opened her eyes and looked at her watch. Forty minutes had gone by! In an instant! She scrambled to her feet and grabbed her things. She looked around for something that was making that weird humming sound. Just as she tried to get her arms around it, everything went quiet. Except for the bees in the rose bush. She shook her head and ran to the elementary school. Eddie and Sarah were standing on the front porch, looking a little forlorn. One of the moms was keeping a watch over them, and she seemed to heave a sigh of relief when Annie ran up to get them.

Eddie said, "Why are you here alone? Where's dad's car? I don't feel like walking. I'm too tired." He dragged himself up to go home.

Annie tried to calm her racing heart. She knew that she had almost screwed up big time, leaving these little guys alone too long, when they were expecting someone to come from them. She told herself that she had to be much more careful about things from now on. She must be tired out from school, but these little guys depended on her. She grinned at Eddie and ruffled his hair, "Well, suck it up buttercup. Dad had some work to do after school to set up a lab. So, here I am and that is the way it is."

Sarah looked up at Annie adoringly. "Well, that's fine with me. Can I watch cartoons when I get home? And have a pudding? I had a really good day. We're starting to read in English class, and I'm already really good at it because you taught me all my letters and their sounds. I'm one of the best readers in the class."

She smiled beatifically, and Annie gave her a hug. "Good for you," Annie said. "You're making us all really proud."

Eddie grumbled, "I'm in the top reading group too, you know. In my class." Annie remembered how it felt to not be noticed.

She said, "Well, I'm very proud of you too. So, you can have pudding or ice cream. Both of you. Let's get home and do our homework, so we don't have to worry about it anymore." They walked the last blocks home together.

While they walked along, Eddie shook his head. He had been thinking. As they walked into the house he veered into the family room and said, "Not homework first, Annie. I can't think anymore. I have to eat and watch cartoons and do nothing useful. Then maybe I can do my homework. But not right away." He slumped down on the floor, right in front of the t.v. He gathered a couple of the big floor pillows and sort of made himself a nest. Then, he lay back with the remote in his hand and tuned out.

"I get it," Annie said. "That makes sense to me. Anyhow, let's get you a snack. Sarah asked for the same thing Eddie was going to have, whatever it was.

"Now you're talking," said Eddie. Sarah plopped down beside Eddie, grabbing a couple other pillows and making her own little nest. When she got comfortable and she thought no one was looking, Sarah slipped her thumb inside her mouth and started quietly sucking it. Annie smiled at the two of them. They were so little, and they were really so brave. She knew that they missed her mom too, but they just kept going, doing the best they could. Being ordinary little kids. That was pretty cool. She felt the weight of the responsibility of watching over them. She knew that it was sacred. Important. She would not be careless about that responsibility again. They both seemed to be doing all right, more or less. And Annie knew that she was doing the best she could too. But she missed her mom so much. She hoped that Eddie and Sarah didn't feel her absence as keenly as she herself did. They were too little to be that sad.

Chapter 7

The next day in English, the class talked about the character of Roger Chillingworth. While Annie was reading the assigned chapters the night before, she had a weird shiver about this character. First of all, his name kind of creeped her out. She wondered if Hawthorne was trying to give them a hint. Maybe he was suggesting that this character is a chilling one. Something like that. In the chapter called, "The Interview," he gets a private interview with Hester and tries to make her tell him who she slept with. He kind of lets her know that it will be his life's mission to find the answer to that question, and that he will stop at nothing until he knows who it is and destroys him. But the weird thing is that when he talks about destroying whoever her lover is, he talks about destroying the man's soul.

Now, Mrs. Murphy started off the day's lecture by talking about the importance of not jumping to conclusions when you read. She said that you need to consider yourself almost like a judge who is receiving conflicting testimony from a wide variety of witnesses. And you sort of sit back and listen to everybody, and when all the testimony is in—only then do you decide. However, Dylan had other ideas, and he wasn't shy about sharing them.

He said, "I get what you mean, and I don't mean to contradict what you say. But I just have a feeling that Dimmesdale is the dad, and he is too chicken to admit it. Because it would knock him off his high and mighty pedestal in the town. He likes everybody to think he's a saint. And I think he's not."

He lobbed this idea up there and waited for Mrs. Murphy to react. She seemed to listen carefully to what he was saying, and she said that his observations showed that he had a good mind, and that she was impressed with his analysis. Again, however, she cautioned him not to rush to judgment. Annie watched the two of them interact and thought to herself, Dylan is not dumb. He dresses like a bad boy, and he struts in here like he owns the place, but he's smart. And he can't hide that. And Mrs. Murphy seems to be the kind of person who doesn't hold a grudge. What happened between them on the first day of school— well, they had started off on the wrong foot. For sure. But it didn't seem to matter at all. The class discussion went on, and Annie listened to everything that everyone was saying, but she kept quiet.

She did take some notes in the margin of her book and underline some passages that Mrs. Murphy said were important, but she did not raise her hand to add anything to the discussion. Soon enough, the hour was over. In fact, it seemed to fly by, and Mrs. Murphy assigned them to read another five chapters tonight. Annie quickly thumbed through her book to see how many pages that translated to, and she thought to herself—that's a lot of reading for tonight. She wondered if she would have time to get it done.

As she was walking out of the classroom, with her arms full of books, Dylan bumped into her. Not hard, really, but hard enough to notice. She looked up at him and resettled her books in her arms. He had really dark brown eyes, with something of a naughty twinkle in them. In spite of herself, she breathed in deeply, almost sharply.

"Sorry," he said. "Didn't mean to spill that pile of books you're carrying."

"Well," said Annie, "you didn't. Almost, but not quite."

"I saw you writing notes in the margins of your book today," Dylan said. Annie said nothing, because she couldn't really think of anything to say. He grinned at her. "Were any of those notes about me?"

Annie gasped. "Of course not. They were about things that I was thinking about the story. That's all."

He brushed past her. "Right," he said. "See you tomorrow." His shoulder brushed hers as he walked away. She felt this weird little electrical charge run through her. It was totally unexpected and very hard to understand. What was that?

Annie ran their whole conversation through her head as she walked to her next class. Now, what in the world was any of that supposed to mean? He wondered if any of the notes were about him? What a strange thing to say? She was going to have a hard time getting her head ready for Geometry.

That day after school, Annie was walking down the hallway and two kids from her English class caught up to her—the handsome, quiet, dark-eyed boy named Brendon and a girl who said her name was Elizabeth. Brendon called out from behind Annie and said, "Hey, Annie. Do you have a minute?"

Annie turned around and smiled and said, "Hi. Yeah. Of course. What's up?"

Brendon said, "I think we have English together first hour, right? Well, anyhow—Elizabeth and I are going to join the cross-country team. Somebody told us that you like to run, and we were thinking that maybe you would like to join too?"

Elizabeth chimed in, saying, "You know that in order to graduate you have to have participated in at least one sport? It's a new commitment to physical fitness or something. Well, we heard that you are a pretty good runner, and we were thinking that you might like to join with us. You know, safety in numbers, and all that?"

Annie smiled. They both seemed really nice. She said, "To tell you the truth, I hadn't really thought about it, but I did like running track last year. I'll talk to my dad and see if he thinks I can work it out with my schedule. When is the first meeting?"

Brendon said, "Tomorrow after school. Right at 2:45. In the gym. I think the coach is really looking for some freshman runners. You know, the future of the team and all that stuff. Hope to see you there." He smiled and then walked away, Elizabeth trailing after him, sort of like an adoring puppy. He moved with the easy grace of a runner. Elizabeth looked like the sturdy little cheerleader type, but it was pretty clear that she could be pretty athletic. Annie herself was long and lean, and she had to admit to herself that she had always wondered if maybe she could run competitively.

Annie was thinking about all of this, and that it might be fun, as she walked down to her dad's classroom to let him know that she was leaving for the day. As she walked into his room, the adoring throng was there. Of course. But, someone else was there too. Mrs. Murphy. Totally weird, thought Annie. Is she there to talk to him about me? He teaches AP Physics and she teaches freshman English. What could they possibly have to say to each other? She smiled and walked over to her dad's desk. Everyone was laughing about something that her dad had just said. It must have been really funny. But that too was weird, because Annie never really thought of her dad as funny at all. Witty—yes. But not really funny. But presumably he was, or at least a lot of other people thought so.

"Hi, dad," she said as she came in the room.

"Oh, hi Annie," he smiled. She walked over to his desk and he put his arm around her shoulders. "I've been talking with your English teacher here." He grinned at Mrs. Murphy.

Annie blushed ferociously. Had she done something wrong? Her mind was racing, but it could come up with nothing.

Mrs. Murphy smiled. "Hi, Annie," she said. "I am so glad that you are in my honors class. It looks like a really smart class we have together. How are you enjoying *The Scarlet Letter* so far?"

Annie sort of felt like she was on the spot. It felt like all the people crowded around her father's desk were waiting for her to say something brilliant. She could only come up with, "I really like Hester so far. And I don't like that Chillingworth at all. He gives me the creeps. I don't know why, but he does." Several of the seniors smiled knowingly, and Annie wondered if she had said something stupid, or something smart.

Mrs. Murphy smiled. "Well, that shows me that you have very good instincts. Anyhow," she turned and smiled at Annie's dad, "I have to be going. See you all tomorrow. Have a good evening." Everyone started to drift away, calling out goodbyes to her dad and to Mrs. Murphy. It occurred to Annie that most of the seniors there probably had Mrs. Murphy for a teacher when they were freshmen. But that was three years ago—almost forever!

When everyone had straggled out, Annie's dad finished packing up his briefcase and said, "Let's go, kiddo. I'll give you a ride home. We'll swing by and pick up your brother and sister." They walked out to the car together.

Annie said, "Was Mrs. Murphy coming to see you about me? Also, I was wondering if I could join the cross-country team. A couple kids in my class asked me if I would like to join with them. And we have to do a sport before graduation, and I like to run. So, I thought I would, if it's o.k. with you." They got in the car, and her dad started it and pulled out of the parking lot. Mrs. Murphy was pulling out too, and he waved at her. She waved and smiled.

Her dad pulled out of the lot and said, "That's really a great idea about cross-country, Annie. I'm glad you're making friends already. Good for you. And it's a good thing to join a sport. It's a way of making a whole lot of friends, because you guys will be in something big together. And the truth is, you've always been a pretty good runner. I guess it's time to see just how good you are." He turned and smiled at her. "And don't worry about your little brother and sister. I know that practice is after school. But, Mrs. Miller, the lady across the street has told me that she could pick the kids up and bring them home to her house until we get home. So, you don't have to do it."

Annie felt a huge relief. Mrs. Miller was such a nice lady. The truth is that Eddie and Sarah would probably love going to her house for an hour every day. Mrs. Miller had two kids of her own, just a little bit younger than Eddie and Sarah. And she baked homemade cookies just about every day. It would be a home run for them to spend an hour with her. Annie said, "Well, there's an organizational meeting tomorrow after school. At 2:45 in the gym. So, I guess I'll go." An idea was nudging at the back of her mind. Suddenly, she remembered. She turned to face her dad. "Hey," she said. "I almost forgot. Did Mrs. Murphy come see you about me?"

Her dad kept his eyes straight ahead, on the road. He cleared his throat softly and said, "No. Not at all. Although she said that she gets the feeling that you are going to be very good at English. But no." He glanced at Annie quickly. "You see. We're friends. She lost her husband five years ago to cancer, and I lost your mom two years ago. As you know. So, we've both been through some pretty rough times. And sometimes it helps to talk about it with someone that gets it." He glanced over at Annie.

Annie was stunned. Almost speechless. She felt the beginning of tears at the corners of her eyes. They had come on so quickly that it caught her by surprise. She didn't know what to think first. Thoughts were wrestling with each other in her head, trying to shove their way into the front of the line. Or at least that's what it felt like. First of all, why couldn't he talk to her about what he was feeling? Secondly, she had lost her Mom—had he forgotten that? Thirdly, it was not possible. Was it? Were her dad and Mrs. Murphy thinking about being more than friends?

Annie looked at her dad, long and hard. She managed to say, "You can talk to me about how you feel, you know. You don't have to keep it all bottled up inside you. It might do me some good too."

Her dad reached over and squeezed her knee, or just above it—her old tickle spot. He smiled, but it was kind of a sad smile. He said, "I know, kiddo. I know I should probably talk more to you about it.

But I never want to burden you with how I am feeling or thinking. You've got your own life to lead. And the truth is, I'm still working things out in my own head, day by day."

Annie said, "But your life and my life are all tangled up together, aren't they? So, I want to know what you're thinking about. And I don't want anything to come between us." That was all she could say. All she trusted herself to even try to say.

He smiled, kind of sadly, and said, "Nothing ever will. Nothing. I love you, Annie. More than life itself."

But Annie thought he sounded kind of sad as he said this. He grinned at her and said, "Since when did you get so wise, anyhow? Our lives are tangled up together? That's really a good line. I like it a lot. I'm a pretty good scientist, but I've also been a student of literature, and I think maybe you have the soul of a poet. You must get that from your mom. She was very good with words. I struggle to write anything, but she used to just sit down and the words would fly out of her fingers. Like she didn't even have to think. She told them to come and they did. She was something." Annie was so surprised to hear him speak like this about her mom that she could hardly breathe. She was afraid to say anything at all, for fear that it would stop the flow of words that were coming out of him for a change. He didn't seem to like to talk about her mom that much, almost as if thinking about her just hurt too much. And she was always afraid to ask him anything. She wanted him to start the conversation, not her. Now, suddenly, however, he stopped. He seemed to have said all he was going to say today. They pulled up in front of the kids' school, got out of the car, and he put his arm around her shoulders as they walked into the after-care room. "Anyhow," he said. "You go to the cross-country meeting. You'll be a good runner, I think. By the way, do you know where the cross-country team does their training? On that old train track you like so much."

Annie shivered just a little. "Really," she said. "Well, that will be cool." The old train tracks. The narrow gate. The rose.

Chapter 8

The next day in English class Mrs. Murphy
led the class in a discussion about the
chapter called "The Minister's Vigil," the
one where Reverend Dimmesdale ascends
the scaffolding at midnight, and Hester and
little Pearl join him in his spooky vigil. As
they stand there together, a gigantic letter
"A" seems to be scrawled across the sky: "a
light gleamed far and wide over all the
muffled sky." It seemed to both
Dimmesdale and Hester that some comet
seems to be inscribing the letter "A" in the
heavens above. Dimmesdale gasps and
Hester does too.

 "Notice," said Mrs. Murphy, "that in
his shock at seeing his guiltiness seemingly
proclaimed by the heavens above,
Dimmesdale places his hand over his chest,
and he seems to be in pain. Remember, we
know that he may have scratched or cut an
"A" into his own chest, to secretly wear the
same brand that Hester must wear. What do
you think of this whole scene?"

 Annie sat quietly in her seat, not
wanting to be the one to answer this
question. She had read the chapter last
night, and she had thought about it before
falling asleep. The way Hawthorne wrote it,
he put in enough little sidesteps that you
could say that the whole thing was just a
figment of their imaginations. But still.

Olivia put her hand up timidly. Mrs. Murphy smiled at her and said, "What do you think, Olivia? Is there an 'A' in the heavens above that night, and is it possible that his secret sin is being proclaimed in this way?"

Olivia seemed to swallow hard before she answered. Annie thought she was very brave to tackle this question. Olivia said quietly, "I know that a lot of people might think that I'm silly. But, I kind of think that this is exactly what is happening. Even if the comet doesn't really make an 'A'—Hester and Dimmesdale see the letter. So, they feel that the heavens are announcing their secret sin. I'm not sure it really is a sin, but they think it is. Now, Hester has already confessed, and she is publicly doing penance. But for Dimmesdale, this is the world telling him that he has to come clean or he will never know peace. I think that sometimes we get little nudges from our world, helping us to make the right decisions." It was clear that Olivia had now exhausted herself with saying this much. Her cheeks flamed, as she seemed to ready herself for an attack from her peers. And, sure enough, there were some titters from the back of the room. One of them was from Dylan.

Mrs. Murphy turned sharply to him. "Dylan," she said. "Watch it. What Olivia has said here is a very valid interpretation of this scene, and many very well-respected scholars would side with her. I take it that you see the scene differently. What would you like to say about it?"

Dylan seemed a little chastened. It occurred to Annie that he didn't want to get on Mrs. Murphy's bad side. Dylan nodded to Olivia. "I'm sorry. I wasn't making fun of her answer. It's a good answer, and I think there is plenty of evidence to support it." Again, Annie realized that, in spite of his gruff manner, he was really pretty smart. He went on. "It's just that I don't really think the natural world cares about us or our sins, one way or the other. I don't know if it was a comet or a shooting star, or something else. Who knows? But I sincerely doubt it scrawled any kind of letter across the sky. That is just not very probable. It's just that, when we've done something we think is wrong, we seem to feel like the whole world knows. And probably, nobody does. Lots of sins go unpunished."

As Annie sat there listening, she realized that both of them had a valid point. Mrs. Murphy went on to say the same thing, but much more eloquently. She said that there are three scaffold scenes in the novel, and that they form a kind of framework for the theme of the story. At this point, they had read about two of them. A final one was coming. Then she said, "Now. Reverend Dimmesdale is hoping that by ascending the scaffold with Hester and Pearl, he has confessed his sin, and he can finally have peace. Does this scene constitute a confession? Why or why not?"

Again, Annie sat quietly, not wanting to be the one to speak first. She scribbled on her notebook, and kept her eyes down. Mrs. Murphy called on her just the same. She said, "Annie. If you had to take a position on that one, what would you say?" Annie felt her cheeks start to burn. She looked up at Mrs. Murphy who was looking at her very kindly.

"Um. I don't think it is any kind of a real confession," Annie stammered.

Mrs. Murphy smiled at her and quietly said, "Why not?"

Annie hadn't really thought that far. She scrambled for an answer. "Well," she said. "It just doesn't seem very fair or equal in any way. Hester had to stand there for three hours, holding her baby in her arms. With the whole town staring at her. And he gets to be forgiven for a secret confession in the middle of the night that nobody witnesses? And he loses nothing by making this secret confession? It just doesn't really seem fair to me."

Mrs. Murphy smiled. "Well, that's a very good point, Annie. However, as you will read tonight, his secret 'confession' does not go unnoticed. There are witnesses, although they don't know what they are seeing. Very good job today, everybody," she said. "For tonight, read the next three chapters, and we will talk about them tomorrow. Now, let's turn out attention to our grammar books. We are going to do a little work on commas, and when to use them." The whole class groaned in misery, and Annie felt herself tune out.

That afternoon, she went into the girls' locker room and changed into her running clothes. The people who wanted to run cross-country were supposed to meet on the track at 2:45. That only gave her fifteen minutes to get all her homework stuff together, get down to the gym, get changed, and get out on the track. Hardly even enough time to run to the bathroom. Anyhow, she made it out there, and there were about sixty kids gathered at the track—lots of kids that Annie didn't know. She did see Brendon, Elizabeth, and Gabriella, three kids she knew from her English class. At the far edge of the group was Dylan, surrounded by a few other guys that seemed to be like satellites in his orbit.

Annie walked over to Brendon. "Hi," he said. "I'm glad you came out for the team. I wasn't sure you were going to." He smiled at her. His hair was brown and thick, and it ruffled in the wind. His brown eyes sparkled in the afternoon sunlight. He was thin, and Annie thought to herself—he is probably really fast. He had very new shoes on, and Annie's shoes were about a year old. To tell the truth, they were probably all beat up inside, and she should ask her dad for new ones. She would try to remember to do that tonight.

The coaches strolled on to the field—Mr. Watson and Mr. Place. They both carried clipboards under their arms. They were wearing tracksuits with the school logo on their chests. They looked impressive, and pretty serious about what they were doing. Mr. Place spoke first. "O.K. everybody," he said. "Thanks for coming out for the cross-country team. As a runner, you will probably be one of the best and, also most under-appreciated athletes in the school. Nobody cares about cross-country meets. Nobody will come and watch you run. Except maybe your moms and dads."

Everybody laughed kind of quietly. Annie thought to herself, not my mom. Sadly. She started to drift in her thoughts, and suddenly Brendon put his arm around her shoulder and gave her a hug. Just a quick one, but Annie glanced up quickly at him. She smiled. "Thanks," she whispered. "I guess maybe my dad will come sometimes. But probably not. He is too busy with the little kids and with teaching."

Brendon whispered, "The truth is that nobody comes to cross-country meets.

You run for yourself. But if you get hooked on running, and you may, it will become a life-long habit. And it will keep you healthier and better looking than a lot of the other athletes from the big-ticket sports who will be soft and broken by the time they're fifty."

Annie could not even imagine being fifty. That number was beyond her imagination. Even her dad wasn't fifty yet. She wondered how Brendon could even think in those terms.

Mr. Place was still talking, and Annie started to pay attention again. "We run 3.1 miles in a cross-country meet. And we run on terrain that can be unpredictable. When we go to other schools, we run on trails that are unfamiliar to us. That makes the whole thing just a little bit tricky. And there can be stumbling blocks—bad earth, with rocks in place. And tree roots sticking up to trip you. It's a lot of fun. Now personally, I think we have a really good route for our runs. We run on the old, abandoned railroad tracks about a half a mile from here. The state has taken out the rails and made us a nice, gravel track. We enter through a narrow gate and run about one and a half miles out, loop around and come back. So, seniors, lead the way. You know the route. And you younger runners, fall in behind. Let's see what you've got."

The seniors, many of whom were quite a bit taller than Annie, started to lope off towards the trail. Annie fell in near the back of the pack. Brendon and Gabriella did the same. They all started off at a very comfortable pace. Soon, they were at the gate, and everybody slipped by it. Although a couple show offs acted like they were going to leap over it. But, the senior runners swung the gate opened, and they all filed through.

The afternoon sun was still warm. Out here on the abandoned tracks, you couldn't hear the sounds of civilization really. No car horns, no doors slamming. Just the sound of many feet scuffling on gravel, people breathing, and talking quietly. It was weird. At first, some people were talking loudly, shouting insults or encouragements at each other, but pretty soon, it settled down into a very quiet run. Annie felt herself loosen up as she went on. She felt her stride lengthen just a little, and she felt her breathing settle in to a steady pattern. She kept her ear tuned to the atmosphere, to see if she could hear that weird humming she had heard here the other day. But she heard nothing strange. Just feet on gravel, scuffing along. And people breathing. Birds twittering in the nearby trees. And the wind. She thought to herself that she must have imagined it the other day. Just like Reverend Dimmesdale and Hester imagined that some star had scrawled an "A" across the sky. Annie must have imagined that weird humming in the air. She forgot all about it then, and matched her pace to the runner in front of her. Before she knew it, she was back at the school and the run was done. Time to head home to her dad and the kids. It had been a good day.

Chapter 9

After dinner that evening, Annie heard laughter coming from the study. Her dad was in there, doing some grading. She tapped on the door, which was shut— surprisingly—and went in.

It was almost dark in there, with only the low-level lamp shining on the computer desk. Her dad was sitting in the desk chair, with his feet up on the desk—leaning back in the chair and laughing! It almost sounded like he was flirting! Annie could not believe what she was seeing. Who was he talking to?

He saw Annie come in and waggled his fingers at her, gesturing for her to come in. Then, he held up a finger as if to say 'just give me one minute.' She sat at his feet, poking at a rose pattern on the Oriental rug that they had inherited from Annie's mom or grandma long ago. Her dad wrapped up his conversation, hung up the phone, reached down and tousled her hair, and said, "Hey, baby. What's up?"

Annie was caught off guard by the whole moment. He seemed almost happy, almost younger for a minute.

She said, "Who was that on the phone?"

He turned back to the computer where he had his grade book open. So, he was grading papers and recording grades.

Without looking around, he said, "Oh, that was Mrs. Murphy. She was having some trouble with the new grade program, and I was able to help her out. What can I do for you?"

Annie thought about that, and thought to herself, his conversation had sounded like he was having a lot more fun than just helping her with some grading program. However, after thinking about the whole scene for a minute, she decided to just let it go. Instead, she said, "Dad, I think I need new running shoes. You know I've started track practice, and today we ran three miles. When I was done, my big toes hurt. I think they're pushing on the top of my shoes. I think I need to go up a size. Can we stop by Miller's Sporting Goods and get me a new pair tomorrow after school?"

"Absolutely," he answered absent-mindedly. "Just remind me and we will swing by there on the way home. Do you have practice tomorrow?"

Annie stretched out on the rug. She could feel her back straightening out. As she lay flat, she noticed that her boobs were finally worth noticing. Not just flat little bumps anymore. But real boobs. Again, she missed her mom. She would have liked to show them to her. She had so many questions about everything. "Are you and Mrs. Murphy good friends?" she asked. The words had just popped out. She hadn't even planned to ask him that.

He cleared his throat nervously and said, "Well. We are kind of becoming good friends. I kind of wanted to talk to you about that. I was thinking of asking her to go to a movie with me. And maybe to get a cup of coffee this weekend? Would you be all right with that?" He was still looking at the computer screen, not at Annie.

Annie felt a roaring in her head. She felt a little faint or sick or something. She was trying to think of what she wanted to say, but nothing was coming out. Instead, her dad spoke again.

"You know, Annie. It's been over two years since your mom died. And Mrs. Murphy is all alone too, and I was just thinking that it might be nice to have a friend to go out with and laugh with. This does not mean that I don't still love your mom and miss her with all of my heart. I miss her every day. Just like you do. And this is nothing serious. No big plan or anything like that. Just dinner and a movie. Just two good friends keeping each other company occasionally." He looked over his shoulder and saw Annie lying on the carpet, her eyes fixed on the ceiling. He seemed to be waiting for her to say something.

A million ideas went through Annie's head. How could you do this to me? And to Eddie and Sarah? How could you do this to Mom? If you were the one who was dead, she wouldn't do it to you? Won't everyone at school be talking about this? Isn't it supposedly a very bad idea to date someone you work with? What will everyone say when this gets out? Does Mrs. Murphy have any kids of her own, and what about their feelings? And isn't it a bad idea for him to date her English teacher? Doesn't that complicate things to an almost unbearable level? And what would Mom say? It seemed like a betrayal of her memory. It seemed awkward and juvenile and risky and wrong.

These thoughts ran like a freight train through her head. She looked at her dad and said, "Do you think this is a good idea?"

He smiled and said, "Well, I don't think it's a bad idea." He tousled her hair again and went back to his grade book. Annie got up quietly and went to her room.

Chapter 10

The next morning, Annie went in and found her desk. She felt totally weird. She looked at Mrs. Murphy, who used to be her favorite teacher—just yesterday, in fact—and realized that she now felt completely different about her. She tried to catch her eye, but she was busy arranging some papers on her desk and getting ready for the day's lecture. The bell rang, and Mrs. Murphy said, "All right everybody. Closing thoughts on *The Scarlet Letter* today. Let's have a look at these last chapters. Let's look at the second to the last chapter, where Reverend Dimmesdale finally makes his public confession. Annie, could you please read the crucial final speech from the Reverend out loud for us?"

Her request caught Annie completely off guard, and she almost choked and sputtered. She felt herself blush all the way to her roots, but she kept her eyes down and found the right page. Pulling herself together, she read the final sentences from Dimmesdale: "God knows; and He is merciful! He hath proved his mercy most of all, in my afflictions. By giving me this burning torture to bear upon my breast! By sending yonder dark and terrible old man, to keep the torture always at red heat! By bringing me hither, to die this death of triumphant ignominy before the people!

Had either of these agonies been wanting, I had been lost forever! Praised be his name! His will be done! Farewell!"

Annie read the passage quietly, but with a strong voice. She felt the majesty of the words as she finished reading. The classroom was very quiet. It seemed like everyone was actually listening to the words she had read. Mrs. Murphy said, "Thank you, Annie. Very nicely done. Now, somebody tell me why Chillingworth is so upset during this very powerful scene. Why does he angrily yell that the Reverend has escaped him?"

A ripple of whispers went through the class. Brandon put his hand up and spoke. "I think that when Dimmesdale finally confesses his sin, he frees himself from the clutches of Chillingworth. And, it seems to me that by suffering this public humiliation that he has been dreading and trying to avoid, he rises above the power that Chillingworth has had over him."

Mrs. Murphy smiled and nodded. "Well said, sir. Well said. Does anyone have anything to add to that? Or any other observations?"

Olivia, the girl who had had trouble with her locker on the first day, raised her hand. Annie had kind of decided that Olivia was a timid soul. But she might have been wrong about that because Olivia spoke boldly now. She said, "I kind of think that Chillingworth is the devil."

Mrs. Murphy's eyebrows arched in either surprise or pleasure. Annie wasn't sure which it was. Then she said, "Very interesting, Olivia. Tell me what you mean."

Olivia said, "To me, it sounds like Chillingworth is working for the devil or maybe he even is the devil. I'm not sure. But, it's like if Dimmesdale had not made this confession, he might have gone to hell, and that would have made Chillingworth happy. And, since he made his confession, he will go to heaven, and so he has escaped the devil after all. Probably."

Mrs. Murphy smiled. "Very clever, Olivia. You have put your finger on a very interesting idea. And there's even more to it than that. There's an old legend that the devil can come to earth and take on a human shape. But he cannot disguise his cloven hooves, the hooves of a beast that subtly announce his beast-like nature. So, often, when there is a character that seems to be hellish, the author might have him wobble or walk uncertainly on his feet, as if he is hiding the cloven hooves of a beast under his boots. Have any of you noticed that, as this novel went on, Chillingworth became more and more twisted, unable to even stand upright? And take a look at his name. It's a compound word, isn't it? What is

Hawthorne suggesting by naming his in this fashion?"

Olivia raised her hand again and said, "That he has a chilling nature. That it would be worth our while to stay away from him. Chilling and worth. Maybe?"

Mrs. Murphy smiled again. She nodded. "Very good. I think that works. Let's take a look at the last chapter, and see what we can learn about Hester and Pearl after Dimmesdale dies. How things turn out for them."

Annie thought about everything she had just heard. Part of her wanted to be angry at Mrs. Murphy. Or, maybe not angry. That was not the right word. But annoyed. Because Annie did not think that it was time for her dad to move on to a new relationship. He was still married to Annie's mom, and Annie couldn't bear to think of her mom being sad by her dad seeing another woman. And then a new thought occurred to Annie. What if her mom would be happy for him to do just that? Annie felt herself tumbling into questions and quickly arrested her descent. She tried to focus on one thing—something that mattered right now. She had to admit that part of her liked Mrs. Murphy a lot. And the way she taught. Confusing.

Chapter 11

She got her new running shoes out of her
gym bag and laced them up in the girls'
locker room, sitting on the wooden bench
that ran the length in between the rows of
lockers. Then she crammed her school
clothes in the locker, locked it, and headed
out to the track, where practice would begin.

It was September in Michigan, and it
was one of those golden days. There was a
crispness to the air, a coolness with a little
bit of warm sun dipping lower in the
afternoon sky. The trees were already
starting to turn colors. You could just see
the first bits of yellow in the poplars and
oaks. A gentle breeze lifted her hair from
the back of her neck, or at least the little
wisps of hair there. Most of her hair she had
gathered up into a pony tail, which was way
more comfortable for running. She had on
her favorite black running shorts and a tank
top, plus a new jog bra she had got her
father to buy for her, saying that her old one
didn't fit right any more. He was so
flustered by the talk of a bra that she could
have hit him up for two or three if she
wanted to, but Annie didn't want to make
her dad any more uncomfortable than he had
been. Anyhow, with the new gear all in
place, Annie felt ready to run. Kids were
milling around on the track, waiting for the
coach to say a few words before they took

off. She noticed Dylan standing at the edge of the group, surrounded by his hangers-on. She almost thought she caught him looking at her for a minute, so she quickly looked away.

Mr. Place walked on to the track. "All right, everybody. It's good to see so many of you out here. Senior captains, please come forward." Two guys and two girls stepped forward, turned around and faced the group. Two stood on each side of Mr. Place.

He said, "These are your senior captains— Tom Kelly, Matt Thompson, Kerry Grimley, and Ashley Fraser. They have been running cross-country for three years already. This is their fourth year running for the school. All of them are at the top of their game right now, and if you're serious about running and doing well, you will find them to be a wealth of good practical information. They will lead you in the run today. O.K. Captains, take them out in a nice easy pace, and then pick it up on the way back. Use the old railroad tracks. Have a good run, everybody. Fall in behind your captains. Go."

Suddenly, everyone was running. Just like that. The captains knew exactly where they were going, and without saying another word, they just took off. Annie was in a panic. She thought there would be a little more talk first, but she was wrong. She scrambled to get herself moving and tried to find some kind of a regular pace. She felt so awkward, and it felt like she was not breathing properly. Rather, she was gulping air and she could hear the sound of her feet flopping. It did not sound like she knew what she was doing at all. She knew that, as a runner, she had good days and bad days. She was afraid that this might be one of the bad ones. She struggled to find her rhythm.

All of a sudden, there was a voice behind her. Soft, but urgent. "Hey. Slow down. You're working way too hard. Just breathe, and lengthen your stride a little. I know you know how to do this. You have good legs. You're a born runner. Just breathe and run."

Annie looked over her shoulder and almost fell down in shock. In fact, she actually stumbled. It was Dylan! He saw her stumble, grabbed her elbow and steadied her. He grinned at her, just a little one. "Hey," he said. "I didn't mean to scare you. I was actually trying to help. Are you all right?"

Annie gulped again. "Yes. I'm fine. I mean I think I am. It just caught me off guard. They went out a lot faster than I thought they would. But you're right. I do know how to run. I just have to remind myself of that." She felt herself consciously trying to lengthen her stride.

"Don't forget to use your arms," Dylan said, running beside her. She matched her stride to his. "Lots of people forget all about their arms when they're running. The truth is, you will feel a lot stronger and smoother if you remember that your arms matter. Look ahead, not down. And just let your body find the rhythm. You see, you're running better already." He grinned sideways at her and then took off, accelerating right past her and about twenty other runners.

What the heck was that, Annie thought? I can feel my heart hammering away, and I don't think it's all because of the running. Don't even think about it, she told herself. He is a bad boy. Everybody says so, and just because he seemed nice for a minute there, you must not get your hopes up. Don't be silly. She settled into the run, remembering to use her arms, just like he said, and she actually did feel stronger. All of a sudden, the group of about a hundred runners approached the entrance to the old railroad tracks. Annie was in a small group at the rear of the pack. There were about twenty runners running with her. She entered the path through the narrow gate. The trees rustled in the afternoon wind, and the birds chirped in the trees. Somewhere, a cicada was sort of screaming its weird old one note song, so Annie knew it was probably about 80 degrees now in the afternoon heat. Her mom had told her that they started to make that noise when it hit 80. Annie didn't know if there was any science to back that statement up, but it was one of those things she believed to be true. Believed it because her mom had told her that it was so.

As she passed beside the narrow gate, she wondered about that strange buzzing she had heard there a few days ago. She listened carefully to hear if any strange noise announced itself to her, but she could hear nothing but the sound of runners breathing, and huffing, and feet scuffing on the gravel path. That and the birds and the wind. The sun was dipping lower in the sky already. But it felt warm and sunny. She relaxed into the run and thought about the weird electrical feeling that had run through her body when Dylan grabbed her elbow. It was nothing to him—he was actually just steadying her after he had startled her. But it didn't feel like nothing to her. It felt like something—that was for sure. She just wasn't sure that she had a name for it.

Then, her thoughts went back to her dad and Mrs. Murphy. What was that all about? They were going out for coffee and a movie this Saturday. Annie was going to watch Eddie and Sarah. Her dad said that he would only be gone for a couple of hours. And he said they could order pizza and a Netflix movie, so watching the little guys would not be a problem. Annie just wasn't sure how she felt about any of this. Yes, her mom had been dead for over two years, and she knew her dad had a right to move on. Still, she was so confused about everything. She felt like if she gave her dad permission to pursue a new relationship, she would be being unfaithful to her mom. And then she remembered that her dad didn't need her permission. He was a grown man, and he was a good man.

Did this mean that her dad didn't miss her mom anymore? That he was ready to move on? How would her mom feel about that? Annie thought that she would like to talk to someone about these questions, but it sure couldn't be her dad. Not when he was right in the middle of all the questions. And it couldn't be Sarah and Eddie. They were too little, and Annie did not want to make either one of them experience any more sadness than they already had. Oddly enough, under different circumstances, one of the people she might have thought about as a possible confidant was Mrs. Murphy. That is, before this had happened. But right now, she was right in the middle of all the questions too. So, that would never do. She was making new friends at school; that was true. But none of them were the kind of close friend she needed to be able to talk about something so personal.

She hadn't really noticed where the run had taken them. In fact, she hadn't really noticed that she had moved way up in the pack of runners. She had been mentally someplace else, but suddenly, she looked around and realized that she was in the top third of the runners. She must have edged past over thirty people without even realizing it. All of a sudden, she noticed that she was only about five runners back from Dylan, who was running smoothly and strongly, his eyes forward and his arms working well. They all narrowed into almost single file to go back through the narrow gate, and into the final part of the run—the part that would take them back to the school track.

Annie felt herself running as well as she had ever run. She concentrated on breathing and using her arms. As she slowed for a minute to take her turn passing through the gate, she thought she heard a faint humming or buzzing. Once again, she almost stumbled, caught off guard by the sound. She caught her balance and looked around. Nothing but the gate and the path and the trees and the birds. She must have imagined it. They finished the run and ended up on the track, sweaty and panting. Lots of runners bent over at the waist, putting their hands on their legs, just above their knees, gasping. Annie felt all right, as she ran a quick assessment of how she was doing. Still, she bent over too, like the others were doing, not wanting to make it seem like she was showing off. Suddenly, there was a hand on her butt, just for a minute. A light tap, or slap.

She whirled around, expecting someone to say, "sorry," or something. But instead, there was Dylan, grinning. "Good run," he said. "I saw where you finished. I had a feeling you might be good at this."

She felt herself blushing right to the roots of her hair, adding more color to her already pink and sweaty face. "Did you just hit me on the butt?" she said to him. He grinned. "Just a congratulatory tap. We runners do that. Nothing more than that. No harm done."

Annie looked hard at him and couldn't decide if he was teasing her or if he was serious. "Well," she said, deciding to give him the benefit of the doubt. "Don't do it again, o.k.? Runner tradition or not."

He grinned at her again, lights twinkling in his brown eyes. "All right, sorry," he said. He was still smiling. He was slightly sweaty from the run, and Annie wanted to lick the sweat from his forehead, just above his eyes. She thought this and then immediately scolded herself for thinking it, all within the space of a second. She glowered at him, saying nothing more, and turning away. But her heart was hammering away again, and her butt felt like it had been branded. She could still almost feel the exact places where his hand had touched her. It was like a series of small electrical shocks were running through her. She was excited and thrilled. Also surprised. And then she wondered if she should be angry. Her thoughts whirled around, coming one after another so fast it was dizzying. She controlled her breathing and turned forward to listen to the closing remarks of the coach who was telling them that it had been a very good first run, and that they showed a lot of promise, but that they had a long way to go.

Annie felt like everyone standing around her must have seen Dylan sort of spank her. It was such a huge thing that everyone must have seen it. She waited for one of the girls to say something to her, but no one did. In fact, it seemed that no one had even noticed. Instead, Dylan was flirting with two other girls, both of them sophomores or juniors. He didn't even look over his shoulder at Annie. He had already moved on completely, not knowing that he had left her heart in a new kind of wreckage as her feet stumbled into the locker room to get her gym bag and head home. She looked over her shoulder as she headed in. Suddenly, he looked over and winked at her. What!

Chapter 12

That Friday, at the end of English class,
Olivia came over to Annie's desk at the end
of the hour. "Hey," she said, smiling. "I
was wondering if you would like to come
over to my house for a sleepover tonight.
Maybe you could help me get my head
together to write this essay for English class.
Plus, I would just like to spend some time
with you." Annie was astonished, and
pleased. All through elementary school, she
had had friends, but never anyone that was
like a best friend. And she was a little bit
shocked that Olivia was seeking her out. It
was widely rumored that Olivia's parents
were really rich and that she lived in a
castle.

Annie said, "Well, I have cross-
country practice, but that doesn't take long.
We just have to run the three-mile course,
and then that's it. But, I have to ask my dad.
Can I get your cell phone number, and I'll
call you? Or, if you want, you could come
down to his room after school with me and
we can ask him together."

Olivia said, "That's a good idea.
Then, if he has any questions about
anything, we can work that out. I can have
my driver wait for you and we can go home
together after your run, if you like."

Annie stammered,
"Your...your...driver? What does that

mean? Doesn't your mom pick you up? Or your dad?"

Olivia shook her head, as she gathered her books from her locker. "Nope. They're both attorneys, and they work later than the end of the school day. So, I have someone who drives me to school. His name is Pierre, and he is about a hundred years old. But very sweet. And he won't mind waiting."

Annie said, "Well, that would be great. I can hardly wait until the day's over now. It will be great to get away for a little bit." She hoped her dad would let her go. Olivia seemed like such a nice person, and it would be good to have a real friend. If it worked out.

Olivia squeezed her hand and said, "Well. Let's meet here right after school and go down to talk to your dad, and then you can go run." Annie agreed and they hurried off to their next classes.

The day seemed to drag on forever, but finally, the dismissal bell rang. Annie met Olivia at their lockers, and together they practically ran to her father's classroom. The adoring throng was there, of course. Annie shouted out, "Dad. Can I talk to you for a minute?"

He smiled at her and held up a finger, so he could finish answering some girl's question about the homework. Then he turned to Annie and saw Olivia. He smiled warmly and said, "Hey, darling. Who is this?" Olivia stood quietly at Annie's side, smiling shyly.

Annie said, "This is my friend Olivia. And she is wondering if I can go to her house tonight for a sleepover? She has a driver, and the driver will wait for me to finish my cross-country practice run, and then we will go to Olivia's. We have a big essay due in English class and we sort of want to bounce ideas off of each other."

"That sounds very nice. No problem. Let me get your number Olivia, and your mom or dad's number, if you don't mind. Am I correct in assuming that you have talked with your mom about this plan of yours and that she is expecting Annie for the night?" Olivia had flipped her phone on, and Annie's dad was entering the phone numbers in his own phone as they spoke.

Olivia nodded. "Yes, Mr. Simmons. I asked permission last night, and I told mom and dad that I could hardly wait for them to meet Annie. She was very nice to me on the first day of school, when I didn't know anybody, and she is one of the smartest kids in our English class. And I could use a little help just sort of gathering my thoughts for this essay. She is also, like I said, the nicest person I've met so far. So, I would really like to have her over, if that's o.k. with you."

Annie could feel herself blushing,
especially since all these seniors were
standing around listening to what Olivia was
saying. It was actually the longest speech
that Annie had ever heard Olivia make. It
kind of sounded like she had been practicing
it before this moment. But her dad just
grinned. He actually seemed very pleased.
A lot of the seniors around the desk had
completely turned to their own issues,
whispering and waiting for her and her dad
to finish up so they could ask their Friday
questions. Her dad smiled and said, "Well.
It sounds like it will be a very fun night for
both of you. If you and your driver don't
mind waiting until her running practice is
over, that would be great."

Olivia said, "No problem. And
thank you sir." Mr. Simmons bent over and
gave Annie a quick kiss on the cheek. Then
he said, "Be home by noon tomorrow.
O.K.?"
Annie said that would be fine, and she and
Olivia left the classroom. The ranks of
students with questions closed in behind
them, just like Moses and the Red Sea,
Annie thought—swamping her poor dad
with their questions before the weekend.
Anyhow, she headed down to the locker
room to get her run in, and Olivia said that
she and Pierre would go get ice cream and
then would be waiting for her in the circle
drive in the front of the school in about an

hour. Annie was thinking how good ice cream sounded, and as if reading her mind, Olivia said, "What's your favorite flavor?"

Annie grinned and said, "I'm almost embarrassed to admit this, because it makes me sound like a really boring person. But vanilla. With hot fudge sauce."

Olivia gasped, "Are you kidding? Not boring at all. In fact, that's my favorite too. See you in an hour."

Annie changed into her running clothes and laced up her new shoes. She felt light and good. Friday night, spending the night in a castle, and then, all of a sudden, she remembered. Her dad was going out with Mrs. Murphy tomorrow night. A movie and coffee, or something like that. She felt her gut tighten up, and suddenly, the good feeling that had washed over her a couple minutes ago was completely gone. Scowling, she headed out to the track, the gathering place.

Mr. Place was there with his clipboard, and lots of runners were already milling around. Some of them smiled at her in a way that they had not done before, and Annie wondered if some of them had noticed that she had had a pretty good run the last time. Maybe. Even some of the upper classmen smiled at her. She found Brendon and Gabriella standing near the back, chatting about the weekend. She went over to join them. Gabriella smiled and said, "Hey. T.G.I.F. Right? What a really nice temperature for a run. Although, I won't mind when we are done with this and the weekend can begin. Don't forget, you guys. We have to write that paper for English this weekend. Which topic are you going to write on?'

Brendon said, "I'm trying to remember what the topics even were. One on Hester. One on Dimmesdale. One on Chillingworth. Is that right?"

Gabriella said, "Yes. And one on images of light and dark. Or something like that. Which one are you going to do, Annie?"

Annie answered honestly, "To tell you the truth, I really haven't given it too much thought yet. I think I might write on Hester, but just mostly because I like her the best of all."

Brendon smiled, "I think I might write on Chillingworth. Just because I despise him. And I like the whole devil or Satan thing. That might be fun. What about you, Gabby?"

She giggled, "Actually, I think I might write on Dimmesdale, because I feel sorry for him. Poor slob. Making such a big deal out of everything. Cutting himself, and driving himself crazy, and all for nothing."

"Well, there you are," grinned Brendon. "A perfect scatter pattern. Except none of us can even remember what the fourth topic was. What are you doing this weekend?"

Annie surprised herself by having something to say, "I'm spending the night at Olivia's tonight. A sleepover. And then, tomorrow night I'm babysitting my little brother and sister because my dad and Mrs. Murphy are going out on a date." She could not even believe that she had just said that out loud. And Gabriella practically choked in response.

"Are you kidding me?" she sputtered. "Wow. On both fronts. First of all, I've got to tell you. Olivia's family is loaded. They live in a castle up in one of the most exclusive neighborhoods around here. I would love to see her house. She seems nice, by the way. Quiet. But nice. So that is very cool. But your dad is going out with Mrs. Murphy! How do you feel about that?"

Annie said, "I really don't know. Her husband died of cancer. My mom died of cancer. Maybe they are forming their own little grief-counseling group. It all feels pretty weird to me. I can't even think of my dad that way. And I am having trouble looking Mrs. Murphy in the eye." She hoped that she had not sounded sarcastic. She didn't mean to, but she was afraid it might have come out that way.

Brendon put his arm around her and said, "Annie. Keep this in perspective. It's just a movie and coffee, isn't it? And you want your dad to go on living his life, don't you? You can't freeze time, and you have got to go on. I'm pretty sure that's what your mom would say if she were here." It always surprised Annie how confident people could be about what her mom would want her to do and all that stuff. Annie wished quietly that she could be that sure of anything. She also kind of wished that she hadn't said anything about it. Would people make fun of her for her dad seeing Mrs. Murphy? But Gabriella seemed to be more interested in Olivia's home.

"Anyhow," said Gabriella. "You have to tell me about the castle on Monday. I have heard amazing stories. You are going to have quite an experience. I'm a little bit jealous." At that time, Mr. Place called everyone to attention. All the runners turned to him.

"O.K. Good afternoon, everybody. Happy Friday. Big football game tonight, and I know a lot of you want to go, so let's get this run in the books and let the weekend begin. Do not do anything this weekend that could result in you getting kicked off this team. Do you understand me?" He looked hard at them and raised his eyebrows for effect. He looked very stern to Annie. Almost scary. Some of the juniors and seniors whispered stuff under their breath or giggled, but the student captains were not giggling. They stood, absolutely stone faced, on either side of Mr. Place, glaring at anybody that seemed to be taking what he was saying too lightly. Annie figured it must be a reference to drinking, but that seemed like a pretty stupid thing for a competitive athlete to be involved in. High school was different than middle school, that was for sure. A whole new ball game.

Mr. Place was still talking, and she forced herself to concentrate. "As you come in to the field, after the run, we will be calling out times, and we will be recording your times for the run. For the first time. So, don't kill yourselves or anything, but this is the first one that we are writing down." Annie noticed, for the first time, that there were about four students with clipboards standing behind the coach, presumably to record the times of all the runners. She didn't think any of them even knew her name. Anyhow, Mr. Place said, "O.K. It's a beautiful afternoon for a run. Take off." Suddenly, all the runners turned around, jostled for position, and took off toward the old railroad tracks.

Annie fell in, somewhere near the back, kind of loping along with Brendon and Gabriella. A lot of the upperclassmen made their way to the front of the pack, leading the rest of the runners on to the old track. As Annie crossed through the narrow gate, she listened hard to see if she could hear or feel anything weird. Nothing. No buzzing, no humming, no vibration. Nothing. She sort of mentally shrugged her shoulders and settled into the run, thinking about nothing. Just feeling the warm sun on her face, and letting the breeze wash over her. She almost felt like she had kind of closed her eyes, even though they were wide open. But, she felt like a nice, warm daze was settling in. Before she knew it, she had lengthened her stride and left Brendon and Gabriella behind. In fact, she moved effortlessly past several runners, many of whom were chatting among themselves, clearly not even really trying. Annie didn't really have anyone special to run with, so she just ran with herself, feeling her strength and listening to her feet on the path. The run was coming easily to her; she realized that she felt very strong and smooth. Suddenly, she was all alone. Well, not really all alone. She could see the senior captains and a few other runners ahead of her on the path. But there was no one beside her. The runners were all strung out along the path, and she had a spot all to herself. She felt herself let go. Weirdly, the old Scottish song started pounding in her brain, but kind of reinvented as a modern song:

> My luv is like a red, red rose,
> That's newly sprung in June.
> My luv is like a melody
> That's sweetly played in tune.

That's as far as it went. Just those lines over and over as her feet pounded on the path. She remembered when she had had a really good English teacher back in seventh grade who told them that some poems had meter. And taught them to put marks over the syllables, whether stressed or unstressed. She felt like her feet were putting the stress marks on every second syllable. Marks in the dirt. She thought back to her mom. It had been over two years now. She felt like she was losing her ability to conjure her up. Her scarf had lost its scent. But luckily, she still had her mom's bottle of unused perfume. She could spray the scarf with it again.

She wished that her mom could see her run. She wondered if her mom was o.k. with her dad going out with Mrs. Murphy. She felt her mind catch on that thought, and then just circle around and around it. My luv is like a red, red rose. Her mom used to sing that so sweetly. My luv my luv my luv my luv. She felt like a broken record, even though there was no such thing anymore. It still seemed like the best simile for what was happening in her head. She was stuck on a thought. Is it all right? Is it all right? What would momma want? She did not even realize that she was running very well. She had made her way up to the front of the pack. She was running about sixteenth, out of a hundred runners. She must have been passing runners without even realizing that she was doing it. She saw that a lot of the runners who were ahead of her were upperclassmen, team captains, and team leaders. She almost stumbled, thinking what the heck am I doing up here?

Suddenly, she felt someone behind her. Just behind her. She peeked over her right shoulder to see who it was. Dylan.

He said quietly, "Don't look back. I already told you that. Keep your eyes forward. Not down, and never back. I've been running behind you for quite a while now. You looked like you were in your own little world. I don't think you even heard me, and I was never more than three feet away."

Annie kind of gulped uncomfortably. "You were behind me the whole time?" she said.

"No. Not the whole time. It took me a while to catch up to you, to tell you the truth. You moved like a ghost or something. Like you were not even touching the earth. Very weird. But I have got to say, the view from the back is very nice. I appreciated it thoroughly." Annie almost fell down as she realized what he was implying. He had been behind her for about a mile and a half, looking at her butt! What the heck? She didn't know if she should feel angry or flattered. Or a little bit of both. But she knew she had to say something to him. But what? They made the turn and started heading back. The upperclassmen cheered and called out encouragements as they passed her going the other way.

Annie said, without looking around. "You are just rude, Dylan. I don't know why you think you are so cool, but stop being such a jerk. It's not going to get you anywhere with me, anyhow." Even as she said it, she could feel herself blushing, adding color to the sweat that was already there, probably making her look even more ridiculous. She felt a little bit proud of herself for saying something that at least sounded tough.

Dylan ran up beside her, matching her pace stride for stride. He looked over at her, grinning. "That is what you are saying, but that is not the truth. Not what you are feeling at all. In fact, there is a part of me that wonders if you actually did know that I was right there, letting me watch your butt and your legs as you run. Knowing that I could not take my eyes off of you." She looked over at him, sputtering.

Annie said, "What are you talking about? You are giving me the creeps! Get your eyes off my butt, thank you very much." She wondered if she was yelling, and if the other runners had heard her.

Unflappable, he grinned again. "They are off your butt right now. Now, they're on your boobs. Also, very nice. Have a good weekend." He grinned at her again. Annie choked, so caught off guard. She almost stumbled, but she caught herself and kept running. Her heart was racing. Dylan took off and joined the top flight of runners, easily accelerating to be in the top ten, leaving her behind. Annie kept running, but she could feel herself steaming—part from the run in the afternoon sun and part from the thrill of, or the shame of, having his eyes move all over her. If she were going to be entirely honest, it was kind of a thrill. She felt strong and sure as she finished the last part of the run, determined, however, not to meet his eyes as she came back into the school track. She passed through the narrow gate, finishing the run without even thinking about where she was, forgetting to listen for any buzz or hum. There was enough of a buzz in her head as it was.

The team managers called out times as the runners came in. Annie heard her time called out. Nineteen minutes and forty-five seconds. That was the fastest she had ever run that course, and she knew it right away. She was definitely in the top group of runners. A couple of the team captains came over to her and congratulated her on her run. They were also talking to Dylan, who had finished ahead of her. A couple of the senior girls were openly flirting with him.

In spite of her promises to herself, she looked over at him, trying to catch his eye so she could snub him. He did not even look her way. She picked up her gym bag and headed out to the circle drive. There was Olivia standing beside a big Mercedes. She grinned and waved. Annie ran over to her and climbed in the big car. Olivia said, "Pierre, this is my friend Annie." He was a big black man with white hair.

He turned around and smiled, doffing his cap. "Pleased to meet you, Miss Annie." Olivia handed Annie a take-out cup with vanilla ice cream topped with hot fudge. "We already ate ours, but we brought you one to go."

"Wow," said Annie. It looked fabulous. She found that she suddenly forgot all about Dylan, the track, the sun, and the run. She said, "I'm sort of afraid that I might be a little sweaty. I don't want to stink up your car."

Pierre smiled gallantly. "I can't smell a thing. Now, Miss Olivia said that you might want to run by your house and get some things because you are staying the night. Is that right?"

Annie said, "That would be great. I'll show you the way. Is it all right if I eat my ice cream while we drive?"

"Wouldn't have it any other way," said Pierre. Olivia settled back into the cushions contentedly.

"Thank you so much. I live in old Rosedale. That's the name of my neighborhood. Go straight for about a mile here."

"What a lovely name. Old roses," said Pierre. Annie settled back against the cushions, smiling. Old roses. My luv is like a red, red rose. The rose by the prison door. Roses, roses. And hot fudge. All right. Enough for now.

Chapter 13

Annie asked if Pierre and Olivia would just
wait a minute while she ran in and got a few
things for the night. No one was home yet.
The little kids must have been in after-care,
or maybe the neighbor was picking them up.
And her dad must have still been at school.
So, she had the house to herself. She tore up
to her room, took a really quick shower, and
slipped into her best pair of black leggings
and a black tank top. Then she grabbed a
hoodie, something to sleep in, and her
toothbrush. She was back out to the
Mercedes in about six minutes flat.

"Wow," said Olivia. "That was
really fast. No wonder you're going to be
such a track star. You must be able to
secretly fly." She smiled at Pierre. He
nodded, started the big car, and they pulled
away.

Olivia babbled happily about the day
and how excited she was to have Annie
spending the night. The town of Old
Rosedale slipped by, and suddenly, they
were in the next town—Bloomfield Hills.
Where the rich people lived. Suddenly, the
houses got bigger and bigger. Most of them
could rightly be called castles or palaces.
Pierre pulled the big Mercedes into the
biggest one of all. It was gray stone, and it
had towers. Real towers, and pillars, and
ivy all over it. Annie could not help herself.

She gasped, interrupting Olivia, without really meaning to, "You live HERE?"

Olivia was grabbing up her backpack. "Yup," she said. "Home, sweet home. Thanks, Pierre." She nudged Annie into action. "Come on. Let's go get comfy. And then we get crazy." She grinned at Annie. "I can't tell you how happy I am to have you here. Ever since the first day when I met you, I've been wanting to hang out with you. Just us. Usually, it's always a group."

"To tell you the truth," said Annie, as they entered the gigantic front hall, "I am really kind of honored. I've never had a best friend before. I have had lots of friends, don't get me wrong. But never a best friend. I just never got picked for that honor."

Olivia grabbed her hand and ran her upstairs to her bedroom. "Well, you just did. Now, let me get comfy too." She took Annie to her bedroom, which was big enough for four of Annie's bedrooms. There was a big four-poster bed in the middle of the room, with a canopy on it. Annie had always wanted a bed like that. And bookshelves and toy shelves all around the room, loaded with books, lots of them from when Olivia was little, but more grown up ones too. Annie saw a hardback copy of *The Fault in our Stars*. She knew that one was very grown up. She had read it last summer. Obviously, this girl was a reader.

And a window seat! Looking out over a beautifully manicured lawn, just sinking into the long afternoon shadows of autumn. Annie thought to herself, "Well, I could be very happy here."

Olivia came out of the bathroom. She too had changed into leggings and a matching top. The whole outfit was Lululemon. Annie recognized it from the new fall catalogue, which she had just about memorized. Olivia hooked up her iPhone to a little Beats pill and put on a playlist she had been working on. They plopped on the bed and stretched out. "So," Olivia said. "What's it like running cross-country with all the upperclassmen on the team. Aren't you intimidated by them?"

Annie said, "No. I'm really not. I don't even really think about the fact that they are so much older than me. Actually, I just kind of run. There are three kids from our English class on the team—Brendon, Elizabeth, and Gabriella. Both of them seem really nice. I can't tell if they are boyfriend and girlfriend, or just friends. They are always together. They even run at the same pace. Oh yeah. And there's also Dylan. So—four kids from our class. I don't know what to think of him. He seems kind of smart in English class, although he sure has a chip on his shoulder. But he was weird to me at cross-country."

Olivia was immediately interested. "Weird how? I think he is a bad boy, that's for sure. But I also think he is very hot. What did he do?"

Annie flipped over on her tummy. She didn't look at Olivia. Instead, she looked out the window in the distance. "He kind of ran right behind me for a while. I don't even know for how long. Then, he sort of allowed me to realize that he was right behind me and had been for some time. Looking at my butt, which he said he liked." Again, she could feel herself blushing, just thinking about it. Also, she was wondering if she should say "butt" or "ass". Why was she even wondering about that? What did that mean? But she didn't have time to pursue that thought because Olivia grabbed her and looked her in the eyes.

"He did what! He said what?" Olivia got the giggles and couldn't stop. "He said that to you. Oh man. I don't know what I would have done. What did you do?" she rolled Annie over and made her sit up.

Annie said, "I just kept running. In fact, I might have tried to speed up a little. But then he ran right next to me and looked at my front. He said something about 'nice boobs' or something like that. I wanted to hit him, but I also wanted to get a good time in since they were recording times for today's run. So, again, I just kept running."

"Wow," said Olivia. "You mean he actually used the word 'boobs'? And also, did he really use the word 'butt'? At least he didn't say 'ass'! Yikes. That seems like he sort of went over the line or something. I don't know what to think about that." Then, she grinned at Annie. "But, you got to admit. It's kind of sexy. Then what happened?"

Annie felt glad to be through that part of the story without shocking Olivia. In fact, Olivia seemed to have just about the same reaction she herself had had. Like, it's not o.k. But o.k. Whatever sense that makes. "Well," said Annie. "Then, I thought I would run away from him, but instead, he put on some afterburner and ran right away from me. I had the best time of my life for the run, but his time was several seconds better. But, you've got to remember that he's taller than me, and he's a guy. I was definitely in the top ten girls."

"Totally weird, but also, at the same time, kind of cool," said Olivia. "I agree with you. I do not know what to make of that kid. He seems pretty smart. But he's got a lot of attitude, and that might get him in trouble. Anyhow, Annie. You can't let him talk to you like that. If you do, he won't respect you. And it is never a good idea to be anywhere near a guy who doesn't respect you." Olivia apparently seemed shy, but there was a good heart, maybe even a great heart in there. Annie felt herself opening up just a little.

Annie smiled at her. "Yeah. You're right. You're right. I know you're right. I'm really glad I talked to you about all of this. It has been rumbling around in my head ever since it happened. I'm almost a little embarrassed to admit that I felt just a little bit turned on by the whole thing. But you're right. He can't talk to me like that. No matter how hot he is."

It felt great to have a friend that she could talk to about something like this. It should have been her mom. Once upon a time, it had been. She had told her mom everything, and she missed her most of all when she needed to talk about something difficult and think it out. At night, sometimes before she fell asleep, she kind of talked to her mom in her head. It felt a little bit like praying. But, it was kind of a lonely way of talking. You didn't really get any responses that you could actually hear. So, it was not like Olivia was as smart or as good as her mom, but she was better than the night's silence. She sort of smiled to herself and wondered if her mom had somehow sent Olivia to her. If you can believe that stuff like that is possible. If so, then maybe the whispered prayers had been heard after all. She wondered if she was being silly to think like that. Anyhow, it was nice to have a friend.

Olivia said, "Wow. What a story. Anyhow, I'm getting hungry. Let's watch a movie. Then, we can order pizza. Then, you can help me get ready to write that English essay. But first, some silly movie. Have you ever seen this old movie called *The Breakfast Club*? If not, then I say that's what we start with."

Annie said, "Never even heard of it."

Olivia said, "Then, get comfy girl. This is a cool story. I guess I would say that it's a little old fashioned. In some ways, a little bit out of date. But, also somehow, still relevant. Kind of dealing with the stuff we were talking about." Just as they were settling in to the movie, Olivia's mom stuck her head in the room. She was wearing a dark blue suit, and she seemed very stylish. And rich.

"Hello, girls," she said. "You must be Annie. I have heard so much about you."

Annie scrambled to her feet. "Thank you for having me to spend the night, Mrs. Wilson. I'm really honored."

Olivia's mom smiled and said, "No. It is we who are honored. Olivia has told us so much about you. Happy Friday, girls. What time do you want pizza?"

Olivia said, "How about around seven or so?"

"Perfect," said her mom. I'll bring it up when it gets here. "Enjoy your movie." Olivia's mom seemed really nice. And young and pretty. Annie felt a brief wave of sadness wash over her, thinking about her own mom and how sick she was at the end. She missed her so much, and sometimes when she saw other kids with their moms, it hurt all the more. It had been over two years now, and people always say that time heals all wounds. Annie thought they were being overly optimistic. She said a quiet hello to her mom in her heart. She had started doing this whenever she needed to connect with her mom, whenever a thought of her crossed her mind or her heart. It helped a little. Annie settled into a big beanbag chair in front of Olivia's big flat screen television. She felt a kind of peace wash over her that was warm and comfortable. Almost like a mom's hug. Almost, but not quite.

Chapter 14

That Saturday night, Olivia was sitting in her room, working on her essay for English class when suddenly her dad knocked lightly on her door and stuck his head in.

"Hey," he said. "Watcha doing?" Annie noticed that he had on dress pants and a good shirt, with a V neck sweater on top. He looked really handsome. She had somehow momentarily forgotten all about his "date" with Mrs. Murphy, but it all came back very quickly. She sniffed the air. He had cologne on.

"Working on my paper for English class. An essay on *The Scarlet Letter.* I'm writing about Hester Prynne and how her character develops through the course of the story."

"Oh, that's right," he said. "I remember you told me that you had that essay due. Well, I happen to be going out for a little bit with your English teacher. Just a movie and coffee afterwards. Eddie and Sarah are both in their rooms, doing their own thing. Eddie is playing video games and Sarah is watching one of her shows on her Ipad. I won't be late. You don't even have to get them in bed or anything. They can stay up until I get back. Just want you to know that I'm leaving for a couple hours, so you know you're in charge.

O.K.?" He came over to her desk and kissed her quickly on the cheek.

Suddenly, it was not all right. Suddenly, everything in her cried out "No!" She swallowed her feelings and felt herself get all sweaty. She wondered if her mom would be all right with this. She looked up at her dad, trying hard not to blink, afraid that if she did, the tears that were forming at the corners of her eyes might fall. She had not been ready for this reaction in herself and felt totally unprepared for the moment, now that it was upon her. Her dad seemed not to notice. But the relevant word might be "seemed". It might be that he did notice, but he didn't know what to do about it or what to say. Sometimes, when he got in that kind of a situation, he tended to just pretend that the uncomfortable thing just had not happened. He turned away and walked back to her bedroom door, saying, "I'll see you in a little bit. Good luck with the paper. Keep a lid on things here."

Annie did not say anything. She turned back to her computer and banged on the keys, putting in a sentence about Hester being an object of ridicule in the opening chapters. She wanted to show how Hester's character never really changed, that she was always a good person, but that the perception of her character changed as the novel went on. This was an idea that she had heard Mrs. Murphy mention, and it seemed like a really good distinction. One worth pursuing. But right now, Annie just couldn't get her mind to it, even though she had been excited to write the paper earlier. Right now, it felt like her mind was jumping all over the place. Instead of writing, she went on Facebook. Her dad had finally let her open an account, and she was just sort of feeling her way into this new world of social media.

She really had not done many posts so far, but she already had about forty "friends," so people were discovering her. Some of her newest requests came from other members of the cross-country team, even some of the seniors and juniors. She flipped through the day's posts and saw pretty people smiling, with their arms around each other. Suddenly, her "messenger" bell dinged, and there was a new message for her. It was from a guy named Preston, who was on the cross-country team. He said that he was having a party for the team next Saturday and she was welcome to come. He said that she should ask her dad, and if he said it was o.k., he would give her the address at school on Monday.

Annie felt her heartbeat race up. Really? An invitation to a party at a senior's house? She knew that she had to ask her dad for permission, but she kind of hoped that he would give in since it was a cross-

country thing. She wrote back and said that
she would love to come. That she would see
him Monday at practice. And thanks. She
grabbed for her cell phone and called Olivia.

"Guess what," she said, as soon as
Olivia answered. "I just got invited to a
party next Saturday by a guy named Preston
who is on the cross-country team with me.
He's a senior! Can you believe it!"

"Oh, my gosh," said Olivia. "You
are so cool. I can't even believe that a
senior knows your name. Wow. Do you
think your dad will let you go?"

"I don't know. I can't ask him right
now because he is out on a date with Mrs.
Murphy. He says it's not really a date, but it
feels like one to me. Just a movie and
coffee. Sort of sounds like a date, doesn't
it?" She swallowed hard. "But anyhow, I
will just tell him that it is a cross-country
event, and that the whole team is going.
Then, maybe he will let me go."

"But is that true?" asked Olivia.

"To tell you the truth, I really don't
know. It might be. If I'm invited, maybe
everyone on the team is. I think I'll just sort
of go with that idea and see if it flies."

Olivia giggled nervously, "Man,
Annie. I don't know about you. You are
getting really brave. Or crazy. I don't know
which." She cleared her throat. "Are you
all right with your dad going out with Mrs.
Murphy. I mean, you know it might be

really good for both of them. They both lost their partners to cancer, several years ago. And I am sure they are lonely. Still. I bet that this is tough for you. You're being really grown up about it." She waited for Annie to say something. That was one of the cool things about Olivia. She didn't talk non-stop. She actually gave you a chance to think about things and then say something back.

Annie tried to gather her own thoughts. "Well, she said. If I'm going to tell the truth, I'm not happy about it. But I don't exactly know why. I want Dad to be happy and to live his life. And I know that Mom is not coming back. And she really loved him, and she would not want him to be unhappy or lonely. I just can't quite work it out. There's some part of me that's mad at him for even wanting to go out with anybody."

Olivia was very quiet for a minute. Then she said, "I can understand that completely." Then she was quiet, again saying nothing. Annie didn't mean to say anything more. She felt like she had already said enough. But suddenly the words spilled out, without her intending to say them at all. "And there's something else, that I can't quite put my finger on. I kind of feel like Mrs. Murphy was mine. My teacher, my friend, my class. And I was doing really well in that class. And now Dad is taking her away from me. I know that this part is completely irrational. But I kind of feel like that too."

Olivia was quiet for another few seconds, as if waiting to see if Annie was done talking. Then, she said, "I get it. I really do. When you first met Mrs. Murphy, there was just your relationship with her as a teacher and a student. And that relationship was very comfortable and you were doing well. And now, this new thing has complicated that, and it doesn't feel the same and some part of you resents it. Is that right?"

Annie flipped over on her tummy, lying on her bed. She nodded her head, even though she knew that Olivia couldn't see her. She said, "That's it exactly. Thank you for understanding." She felt tears creep into the corners of her eyes again. She wiped them off with the back of her hand.

"Hey," said Olivia. "What are best friends for? I really can't even imagine how mixed up you might feel about all of this. I sure would." Annie felt herself grinning, almost in spite of the tears that still wanted to come. "Anyhow, how about a little help with that English essay. We had so much fun last night I forgot to pick your wonderful brain. Which I fully intended to do."

"No problem," said Annie. "Which essay are you writing?"

"The one on Dimmesdale," said Olivia. "I still find him the most important character, and the most interesting character in the whole story. If you could just help me organize my thoughts, or think about what I should write about, I know I can take it from there."

Annie said, "Sure. Let's think about the most important moments for him in the story." She lost herself in the pure joy of thinking about another character and the big moments in his life. Somehow, it helped her not think about the big moments that might be happening in her life. Like a party at a senior's house. Next Saturday.

Chapter 15

Annie had talked her dad into letting her go. She still couldn't believe she had pulled it off. He insisted on driving her to the party. That was embarrassing enough, since almost everybody else was old enough to drive themselves there. It was in a gated community, and they had to give their name at the gate to be admitted. Her dad made her check over and over to make sure that she had her phone and that it was fully charged. He told her that she had to leave by eleven, and that he would be there to pick her up. The only way that she had pulled it off was to tell him that it was a cross-country team event, but she was pretty sure that that was not entirely true. True, there were a lot of people from the cross-country team that were going. But, also true that not everyone on the team had been invited. In fact, only a few freshmen had been invited. She was one of them. Her father pulled up to Preston's house and dropped her off, with further admonitions about being careful and everything. And reminding her again that he would be back by eleven, and she had better be waiting at the curb for him. He kept saying that he would like to come in and meet the parents, or at least be sure that they were actually there. Annie told him, over and over again, that that was not necessary.

She practically begged him to trust her to do the right thing. Finally, he relented.

"I got it, Dad," she said over her shoulder, as she practically exploded out of the car. "I will be safe and I will see you at eleven. Thanks for the ride."

She practically ran up the lawn to the backyard, where everybody seemed to be gathering. There were all kinds of white twinkle lights in the trees overhead, a beautiful swimming pool with all its lights on, and about sixty students milling around on the brick courtyard surrounding the pool. Over in the corner there was a table where drinks were available on a self-serve basis. Everybody had a red Solo cup. She wasn't yet sure if they were drinking alcohol, but she had the funny feeling that they were.

She knew that she looked pretty good tonight. She had her black leggings on and a black crop top. She had had a T-shirt on over it, but she pulled that off after her dad pulled away from the curb. She stuffed it in a bush in the front yard, reminding herself to pick it up before she left. She had pulled her hair up in a high ponytail, letting just a few wisps frame her face. When she ran, she could feel her ponytail tickle her bare back. She felt light and strong and almost kind of sexy.

When she walked into the backyard, she felt the eyes of a lot of the guys and even a lot of the girls rake over her for the

111

first time. It was a very weird new feeling, but she had to admit to herself that she kind of liked it. She had always thought of herself as a little girl. Until recently. But she was starting to be aware that those days were over. Preston spotted her and walked over to her. He had a red Solo cup in his hand, and she could tell it was beer. He said, "Hi, Annie. Glad you could join us. Didn't know if your dad would really let you come. Some people are drinking beer, but you don't have to." As he spoke, he slipped his arm around her waist, leading her over to a group of runners that she recognized from the practices. This totally weird shiver ran up through Annie's spine. She had never felt a man's hands on her bare skin before, and it was like an electric current had run through her. Preston must have felt her involuntary shiver, and he grinned knowingly. He hugged her close for a minute, pressing her to his chest. He felt big, and strong. Again, a totally new sensation. Annie wondered what he was thinking because he was looking down at her and he was grinning. She felt herself blush.

He said, presenting her to the group, "We've got a young one here tonight, you guys. So, behave yourselves. She is a very fast runner, but I do not think she is a very fast person, if you know what I mean." He smiled at Annie and said, "Now you, behave yourself." He grinned and walked away. The group of runners made room for Annie and let her become a part of their circle. They were actually talking about running times. One of the senior girls, whom Annie recognized as a team captain, said, "You had a really good time in that last practice, Annie. Do you think you can beat that, or did it feel like that was pretty much it for you?" As Annie looked around the circle, she noticed that Dylan was standing almost directly across from her. He was looking at her with a strange and powerful intensity, not saying anything. He suddenly realized that she was looking back at him, and his face split into a wide grin.

"I think that Annie can go even faster," he said. Annie was shocked at how comfortable he seemed with the group. She wasn't even sure she could speak, and here he was, holding court. He said, "I ran up behind her at the last run, and I think she was just loping along, not even trying. Of course, time will tell." He grinned at her again and she felt her heart racing. She looked down at her feet because she could feel herself blushing again. She looked back up to see that the group had moved on, but that Dylan was still looking right at her. Suddenly, everyone was dancing. Somebody handed her a red Solo cup and said 'Drink up.' She knew that she was not supposed to drink at the party, no matter what anyone else did, so she smiled and shook her head. But it was cool to be asked. She started dancing with a group of runners that she recognized, and then all of a sudden, she felt out of place. She started to leave the dance floor, or what was working like a dance floor, the brick patio around the pool, when strong arms grasped her and pulled her back. She spun around to see Preston grinning at her. He said, "This dance is mine." Annie panicked. She did not know how to dance with a boy. Or a man. Somehow, he must have known, because he smiled and said, "Just let yourself go loose. I'll do all the work." He pulled her tight against him, and started to sway. She was pressed against his body, from her neck to her feet, and he did do all the work. She felt like she was floating. He whispered in her ear, "Baby, you are so hot, and you don't even know it. That makes you even hotter."

Annie had the distinct impression that she had heard those very words before, and it took her a minute to realize that they were almost the lyrics to a popular song. He probably stole them from the song, but it did not make them any less effective. Slowly, Annie became aware of the fact that there was something hard pressing into her back, and she knew what that meant. She started to pull back just a little, and he pulled her in tighter. "You feel me? You feel me? Baby, it's just about time for you to grow up."

Annie was excited, but also just a little bit terrified. He was so strong, and she could not get out of his arms. Suddenly, someone came up behind them and tapped Preston on the shoulder. Dylan. He said to Preston, "Hey, buddy. My turn. There are four or five senior girls waiting over there for you. This one is too young for you, but those girls know what they're doing, and they want to do it with you." Preston grinned at Dylan. "Thanks for the heads up, man. Not polite to keep the ladies waiting." He gallantly handed Annie off to Dylan, who pulled her into his arms, danced her over to the edge of the dance floor and released her.

"Hey," Annie said. "I'm no baby. He wasn't hurting me." She felt a little embarrassed and a little relieved.

"Not yet, anyhow," said Dylan. "What time do you have to go home? I bet you have a curfew, don't you?"

Annie glanced down at her watch. It was already 10:30. Where had the night gone? All of a sudden, somebody pushed Preston in the pool. It was late September, and the water must have been freezing. Annie gasped, but he came up laughing and sputtering. He scrambled out of the pool and grabbed one of the senior girls and pulled her in with him. She screamed, whether from cold or mock horror, Annie did not know. But she really didn't seem to mind what he had done. Soon they were kissing and rubbing their hands all over each other, and everyone was watching them and laughing. The girl was beautiful and dark, with a great body. Annie recognized her as a fellow runner, but she did not know her name. The girl threw her head back and laughed, with her legs locked around Preston. Annie had the weird impression that they were performing for the audience that was eagerly devouring the scene. In fact, about twenty people suddenly had cell phones in their hands, filming them. Then, another girl got pushed in. All of a sudden, Annie felt way out of her depth. She blushed furiously and told Dylan that she had to go to the front of the driveway and wait for her dad. It was almost time for him to pick her up.

He said, "I'll walk you out there so you don't have to stand out there alone. You never know what might be lurking in the shadows on a Saturday night."

Annie said, "You don't have to do that. Really, I'm fine." She was thinking about her T-shirt that she left in the bushes. She didn't want Dylan to see her retrieve it and realize that she had changed what she was wearing after her father saw her last. However, he insisted that he was coming with her, just until her dad got here. She tried to find the person whose house this was, to thank him for the invitation, but the party had ramped up to another whole level, and he was nowhere to be found.

So, she started out to the front yard, searching for her T-shirt in the bushes and slipping it over her head. As she did so, Dylan grinned at her.

"What," she said. "I was too hot."

"No," said Dylan. "I think you were just hot enough."

Her dad's car pulled down the street and she ran out to meet him and climb in the front seat. When she looked back to wave goodbye to Dylan, he was gone.

Chapter 16

She climbed in the car, and her dad gave her a good, long look. "How was the party," he asked guardedly.

"It was fine. There were a lot of runners there," Annie answered, keeping her eyes straight ahead. "Some of the kids actually were going swimming." She kept her voice nice and even.

"Was there any drinking?" her dad said. He kept his eyes on the road because traffic was pretty heavy, but he kept glancing over at Annie. She wrestled with her answer.

"Yes. There was drinking. Mostly beer. I think they had a keg over on the far side of the dance floor. But I didn't drink anything, so don't worry."

"Annie, I don't even think you should go to these parties. You know that I cannot have you drinking. I teach at the high school, and it would look really bad if a teacher's kid is caught drinking at a party. You just can't do it. I know this makes things hard for you, but honestly, my job is really important to our family's welfare, as you know, and to me personally. And, whether it's right or it's wrong, your behavior has an impact on me."

"I know, I know, Dad," Annie said, too quickly. "We've had this conversation about a hundred times before. I get it.

Actually, somebody offered me a beer, but I just said no, and nobody pushed it."

"Were lots of kids drinking?" her dad asked, his eyes still carefully forward.

Annie said, "Look, I'm not gonna lie to you. It looked like a lot of people were drinking. But not everyone. And it also looked like no one was forcing anyone to drink that didn't want to. Maybe that's just the way it is. But, I know the rules, and I'm not going to do anything to jeopardize your job." Even as she was speaking to her dad about the problem of beer drinking by students, her mind had slipped back to a much more pressing idea. The idea of a man's hands on her bare skin, the way she trembled, the way she had made Preston hard, the way the senior girl (whoever she was) locked her legs around Preston's waist and leaned back, laughing as he ran his hands over her in the water, the way everyone was looking at them and enjoying it. The whole thing was so much more intoxicating than beer. Dangerous and tempting. And very hard to put out of her mind.

They arrived home and Annie thanked her dad for the ride. She gave him a quick kiss good-night and ran up to her room. She wanted to call Olivia and tell her all the things she had seen and felt tonight. She had to tell someone, or she thought she might explode.

Olivia answered right away. "Tell me everything. Start at the beginning and don't leave anything out. I've been waiting for you to call." Annie noticed that it was almost 11:30. She slipped out of her clothes and into her pajamas. She took her hair out of the ponytail and messed it up with her hands. Then, she flopped on her bed and let her thoughts drift back over the night. Olivia said, "Was everybody drinking? Did you drink?"

Annie said, "No. I mean yes. I mean lots of people were drinking, but I didn't drink. With my dad being a teacher at the school, it just is not a good idea for me to drink at any party. He has threatened me with being grounded for life if I do that. But, the weird thing is—I didn't have to drink. I was so excited to be there. The weird thing is that a lot of the runners were there, and they seemed honestly glad to see me. And I felt a little bit more grown up hanging out with the older kids. And there was this one guy, a senior name Preston Ripley, who grabbed me and was dancing with me and put his hands like all over me and was telling me that I was so hot, and I could feel him getting really hard, where he was holding me against him, and…"

Olivia almost screamed, "You did what? You felt what? He did what? Start all over!" She was laughing and screaming and sputtering, all at once.

Annie giggled in return. It felt good to tell somebody, and she sure couldn't tell her dad this. So, this is what it feels like to have a best friend. It was a good feeling. She started all over, and as she described the night, it felt even more magical than it had while she was there. Nothing really happened. Nothing at all. But, she still felt as if she had crossed some invisible bridge, or been given a glimpse of what was coming. She told the story over and over to Olivia, who couldn't get enough of it.

Then, finally, she realized that it was past midnight, and she and Olivia said goodnight. Olivia said that she could hardly wait to see her at school on Monday. Annie grinned and thought that she could wait. She needed to catch her breath after her Saturday night. She turned out her light and put her phone on silent. As she curled up on her side, she could still feel Preston's breath hot on her neck, and his hands on her back. She felt like she had been secretly branded by his touch.

Chapter 17

She walked into school on Monday
morning, and she sort of waited for someone
to notice her in a special way, or to talk
about Saturday night. But it was as if
nothing had happened. She got her books
out of her locker and sat in her desk. She
saw Dylan come in with a couple other kids,
and he never even looked at her. Only
Olivia seemed to have any awareness of the
magic of Saturday night, and for her, it was
all second-hand information, at best.
Anyhow, they took their places as the bell
rang for homeroom, and Mrs. Murphy took
role. She didn't look at Annie either, and
Annie had been all worried that things might
be different between them now that she and
her father had been out on a date. But, it
must not have made much of an impression
on Mrs. Murphy because she did not even
look at Annie in a special way or
acknowledge that anything was different.
When first hour English class began, Mrs.
Murphy said that she was introducing a new
book.

    "Good morning, everybody," she
said. "Please turn your essays in right now.
You may place them in the open folder at
the front of my desk. Make sure that your
name is on the paper. Thank you for your
hard work this weekend." Everybody got up
and moved to the front of the room to turn

their papers in. As Dylan walked by her desk, he grinned at Annie. He had that lopsided grin that had a bit of a naughty feeling to it. Annie felt herself blushing again. Dylan walked back to his seat.

Mrs. Murphy seemed completely focused on what she was going to teach. She said, "All right. It's time for me to introduce our second novel of the year. We are now going to read Ernest Hemingway's novel entitled *The Old Man and the Sea*. It's in the bookstore waiting for you. Please stop by and buy it sometime today, and for tonight, read the first twenty pages." The class groaned softly. "By the way, I do not want you reading any digital copies of the book. I want good, old-fashioned paper. However, if you have an old copy of it at home, and you may have, you may read that. Many of your parents probably read this book in high school or college, so feel free to ask them if they have an old copy before you buy it."

One kid, who sat near the back, said, "It sounds thrilling. A book about an old man and a big fish, I think that's what I've heard."

"Well, Wyndham. It is thrilling, but in a quiet way. I taught your older brother a couple years back, so I am assuming that he has told you something about it. But, as I recall, it was one of his favorite books, so if you ask him about it, I am sure that he will tell you that it is about way more important ideas than that." Wyndham seemed to be put in his place, and Mrs. Murphy addressed the class again. "Please take out a sheet of paper or a notebook and copy down some of the ideas I want to share with you by way of introduction." Everyone scrambled to get paper and pen ready, because when Mrs. Murphy started, she got going pretty fast. Annie grabbed her black marble composition notebook where she liked to keep all her notes for her English class. She thumbed past all the notes on *The Scarlet Letter*, which now seemed like an old friend, and got ready to hear about Hemingway. She knew that Hemingway was one of her mom's favorite authors. That was easy to see because, in the study at home, there were a lot of Hemingway books all lined up together. Annie realized that she could read her mom's copy of this novel, and maybe her mom had left notes in there, which would be really cool.

Mrs. Murphy said, "Hemingway was born in 1899, and when he was only nineteen years old, he went over to Europe and volunteered as an ambulance driver for the Italian army in WWI. He was badly injured there and spent several months in a military hospital. He never fully recovered from these injuries, and having taken machine gun fire across both his legs, he was never as strong as he had been before.

Just imagine if that had happened to you. Anyhow, from this experience, and from his observations of other young men in the military hospital, he got his central metaphor. This metaphor will inform all of his work. Now write this down. And get it right." Annie looked around the room, and everybody was scribbling pretty furiously.

Mrs. Murphy said, "Here it is. Life is a battlefield, and everyone is eventually wounded—either physically, spiritually, emotionally, or intellectually. I suppose you could even be wounded financially. And eventually, you will receive what Hemingway calls a 'sacred hurt'. What is that? It is a hurt or a loss that is so significant and so powerful that it causes you to reevaluate everything." Annie gulped. She looked up at Mrs. Murphy, who was looking right at her. Their eyes met. Just for an instant. Then, Mrs. Murphy went on. "Some of you sitting in this room today, young though you are, have already received a sacred hurt. There is no minimum age requirement, unfortunately. Some of you have lost an immediate family member—a mother, a father, a brother, a sister, even a grandparent or a very close friend. You feel their absence in your life every day. Some of you have had an illness that has compromised your health, or perhaps it has happened to someone in your family. And, as a result of this illness or injury, a whole host of things which once seemed possible no longer are."

Mrs. Murphy spoke slowly now. You could hear a pin drop in the classroom. Everyone was listening intently. A few kids had stopped writing anything. They were just looking at her. Annie suddenly realized that there were twenty-five kids sitting in that room, and that she had mistakenly thought that Mrs. Murphy was speaking only to her. She looked around the room and saw everyone's eyes fixed on Mrs. Murphy, and suddenly Annie realized that there were twenty-five stories out there she had not yet heard. Annie had been thinking that she was the only one carrying around a secret hurt. She was rethinking that assumption now. Besides that, she liked the idea that she finally had the right words to describe it. A sacred hurt.

Mrs. Murphy seemed to wait a minute for her words to sink in. She spoke softly now, but there was no need for her to raise her voice. "A sacred hurt can come in many different forms. It could even be a divorce. Some of you have seen your parents go through that. And it feels like everything you ever thought you knew is in shambles. The future you saw for yourself, the bedrock you built your life's assumptions on has been cracked. And it has crumbled." She knew that they were all listening very carefully. She used her power

126

gently. "So, what do you do when this has happened to you? You can't run from it. People have tried this many times, but it does not work. You run to a new place, hoping to make a fresh start. But the problem is, you take yourself with you." Annie noticed a couple kids nodding their heads slowly.

Mrs. Murphy went on, "You can't drink the problem away, or drug the problem away. The thing about that is, eventually you sober up, and nothing has changed. It might even be worse because you let it get worse while you tried for a temporary escape. And sometimes, if taken far enough, the drinking or the drugs can become a whole new problem. There is no solution there." Again, Annie noticed a couple kids nodding quietly. Others had dropped their eyes to their notebooks and seemed lost in thought.

"Finally," said Mrs. Murphy, "you can't lie to yourself about it or tell yourself not to think about it. These solutions are not solutions at all. First of all, if you lie to yourself, you know you're lying to yourself. And so, you despise yourself for doing so. And if you tell yourself not to think about something, it's pretty much the only thing you can think about. Right?" Annie heard a rueful chuckle from the back of the room. "So, what do you do?" Mrs. Murphy let the question hang there. No one spoke.

She answered herself, "You allow yourself to grieve for your loss. You confront it, admit it, and allow yourself to feel it in all its depth, in all its sorrow. You allow yourself to acknowledge your loss. This is a step that a lot of people want to skip. They think it's unmanly or immature somehow. Or not a good idea. However, not allowing yourself to grieve for your loss just delays the bill. You have lost something or someone, and the world will never be the same again. That is something worth feeling, in all its power, in all its powerlessness."

She took a deep breath. It seemed like everyone in the class was holding his or her breath. Eyes were locked on her. She looked very pretty and very kind today. Again, she spoke softly. "Then, after an appropriate time of grieving, and fully acknowledging the loss, you pack it up in a corner of your heart. Knowing that you will live with this loss until your dying day. And you decide to live. You decide to live your life with gusto. To appreciate every day and every blessing that comes to you. To enjoy dark chocolate and pizza and good wine, and," here there were giggles. She giggled too. "Oh, not good wine. Not yet. Not for you. I think I was talking to myself for a minute. But you can fill in the blank there for yourself. Think of your favorite food, or your favorite cotton blanket and an afternoon nap, or a warm hug from someone you love, or—you get the idea. Until you come to terms with your 'sacred hurt,' allowing yourself to grieve for your loss and admitting that the world will never be the same, until you get past that, you cannot fully live."

She swallowed hard. Still, she was speaking so softly. "So, young though you are, many of you have experienced a sacred hurt. As you probably know, I have experienced one too. So, we will take this journey together and see what one of the greatest novelists of all time has to teach us about how to live our lives. All right? Stop by the bookstore before you go home, unless you know you have a copy at home waiting for you. Read the first twenty pages tonight. We will talk about them tomorrow. Now, take out your grammar workbooks. We are going to spend just a little time reviewing subject-verb agreement problems and their solutions." Now, the whole class really did groan, seeming to come back to earth after an amazing moment of heartfelt communication. Annie felt like it was one of the best lectures she had ever heard. She couldn't wait to start the book tonight. She looked up at Mrs. Murphy to find her smiling right at her. Annie smiled back.

Chapter 18

That night, Annie read the first twenty pages
of *The Old Man and the Sea.* She had found
her mom's old copy in the study, right
where she thought it was. She knew her
mom's handwriting as well as she knew her
own. In fact, she tried to write just like her
mom, letting her notes in the margin blend
with those left behind by her mom so many
years ago. In the first few pages, she found
a line that she really liked. It was describing
Santiago, the old fisherman who was the
protagonist of the story: "Everything about
him was old except his eyes and they were
the same color as the sea and were cheerful
and undefeated."

  She had a feeling that line was
important. It became clear to her that the
old man felt very, very alone in the world.
He had been declared unlucky by the
village, since he had gone out eighty-four
days without catching a fish. His only
friend was the little boy Manolin, whose
parents really didn't want him to hang
around with Santiago. They were afraid that
Santiago's bad luck would rub off on their
son. But the little boy loved the old man.
Hemingway had her hooked already.
Suddenly, her cell phone rang. It was
Olivia.

  "Hi," said Annie. "How are you?"

"Good," said Olivia. "I just finished reading the English assignment. Did you start it yet?"

"I'm just doing it right now," said Annie.

"Oh, well," said Olivia. "I'll let you get back to it. But I wanted to ask you if I could come spend the night with you this Saturday, at your house, I mean."

Annie sat up on her bed and cleared her throat. "I think so. I'll have to check with my dad. But, wouldn't you rather that I came to your house. My house is nowhere near as cool as yours." Annie was thinking about how small her bedroom was, and how crowded her closet, and the kids' toys all over, and the kitchen too small.

Olivia was insistent. "Define cool. What you think is not cool might be what I think is very cool." Annie was once again taken aback by how clever Olivia was. It was easy to underestimate her because she tended to be very soft spoken. But when she had something to say, she said it. And it made you think.

"Well," said Annie. "I will check with my dad and let you know at school tomorrow. If you would like to come, I would love to have you. If you don't mind a mess, and two little kids that will follow you around like little puppies. Eddie and Sarah. They are six and eight years old." Annie knew that Olivia was an only child, and she worried that she didn't really know what she was getting herself into.

Olivia laughed, "That sounds awesome to me. I'm really looking forward to this, Annie. Anyhow, I have geometry to do. I'll let you get back to the old man, and I'll see you tomorrow."

Annie went back to her reading, hoping that this visit from Olivia worked out all right. Her house was nothing like Olivia's. Not even in the same universe. She went back to her reading. There was this very cool conversation about baseball between Santiago and the boy. Santiago admired the great Joe DiMaggio, who played for the Yankees. Annie did not know enough about baseball to know much more than that. But she had heard her dad mention his name as one of the greatest players to ever play the game. Even though her dad was a diehard Detroit Tigers fan. But it was clear that Santiago admired the great Joe DiMaggio immensely. Annie made a note in the margin and determined to watch that image and see if it mattered. Her mom had made a little star there, so she suspected that it did.

That night, she asked her dad if Olivia could come spend the night on Saturday, and he said that would be great. He said that he and Mrs. Murphy were going to a movie, and that Olivia could help Annie babysit the little guys. Annie was surprised that he was following up with another date so quickly. She raised her eyebrows at him, but either he did not notice, or he pretended not to notice. He said that they could order pizza and make a special night of it.

That Saturday night, Olivia was dropped off at her house by Pierre, who guided the big Mercedes into their driveway. Annie ran outside to greet Olivia, and she said hi to Pierre, who tipped his cap to her. Then, she and Olivia waved goodbye to Pierre and came up Annie's front sidewalk. As they stepped into the house, Eddie and Sarah were waiting for them. Annie introduced them to Olivia, and Olivia threw her bag in Annie's bedroom.

Eddie said, "Do you want to play Clue? I have the board game." He looked at Olivia hopefully.

She said, "I would love to play Clue. But I've got to warn you, I'm pretty good at it. It's just about my favorite game." Eddie got out the game and set it up on the living room floor. Sarah crawled on to Olivia's lap and said, "Can I be your partner, because I don't really get how to play this game, but I could be a good partner." She snuggled herself into Olivia's arms and Olivia seemed very happy with that.

"You bet," said Olivia. It will be you and me against your brother and sister." Just then, Annie's dad came in the room. He looked really handsome, Annie had to admit. He had on black pants and a pale blue dress shirt. Annie sniffed the air. Was he wearing cologne?

He said, "Hi, Olivia. I'm really glad you could be here tonight to help Annie handle these ruffians. Annie, here's money for pizza, when you guys are ready. The number is on the fridge. I won't be late." He ruffled Eddie's hair and bent down to kiss Sarah and Annie on the cheek. "See you soon."

He actually seemed happy to Annie. There was a lightness to his step that she hadn't seen in a long time. He went out to the door to his car without even a backwards glance. Annie considered this and tried to decide what it all meant. But not for long because the Clue game was heating up. They played two games, ordered pizza and watched a movie.

At about eleven, she and Olivia tucked both Eddie and Sarah in bed. The kids were both tired and went without much complaining. As they tucked Sarah in, she put her arms around Olivia's neck and gave her a big hug. Olivia seemed almost a little bit choked up. Eddie asked if he could play his hand-held video game in bed for a little while, and Annie said all right, but not for long. Eddie let her kiss him goodnight on the forehead, and as they were leaving his bedroom, he called out, "Goodnight, Annie.

Goodnight, Olivia. It was fun playing games with you."

Olivia was beaming. "You're so lucky to have a brother and sister," she said to Annie. They took turns going to the bathroom and pulling on their pajamas. Then, Annie turned down the covers on her bed. Her copy of *The Old Man and the Sea* was still lying on her bedspread. Annie said, "It's not a very big bed. I'm afraid we might be a little bit squished in here."

Olivia scrambled in and said, "On the contrary. I think it is just the right size." She picked up the copy of *The Old Man and the Sea* and looked at it thoughtfully. "I see you are a little bit further than I am. But I'm enjoying it," she added. Just then, they heard the front door open and her father came in. It wasn't even midnight yet.

"Anybody awake?" he called.

"We are," Annie answered. He walked in her room, smiling. "Did you have a good time?" she asked.

He nodded and smiled. "I did," he said. "Did you guys have a good night? Did the little ones behave for you?" He smiled at Olivia.

She smiled back and said, "I had a great night. Thank you for letting me come over. The little guys were great. We played Clue and watched a movie. They are really cool kids."

Annie said, "We just tucked them in a couple minutes ago, so you might be able to catch them still awake and give them a goodnight kiss." He smiled and said that he would check on that and thanked them once again.

"He's really nice," said Olivia wistfully. Annie realized then that she had met Olivia's mother, but she had not met her father. She wondered about that. They climbed in bed and turned the light off, with no intention of falling asleep. Just of lying in the dark and talking for a while. Still, the night started to work its magic.

Annie said, "I'm sure your dad is nice too," kind of feeling the waters.

"Oh, he is," said Olivia. "He's just kind of screwed up after what happened to us." Annie wondered what she was talking about. She knew that Olivia's parents were both successful lawyers, and they clearly had a lot of money.

"I don't know what you mean," Annie said softly. "What happened to you?" For a while, Olivia didn't say anything at all. Annie had the good sense to wait quietly.

"I had an older brother. Named Darren," Olivia said softly.

"Had?"

"Yes. He died about three years ago. He was a senior in high school, so he was about seven years older than me. But I loved him a lot. He was my hero."

"What happened?" Annie said.

"He got into drugs and got really screwed up. He had so much potential too. He was a National Merit Semifinalist, and a really good swimmer. But, one night, he was too high, and he drove his car right off a highway ramp. He missed a turn, and he was going way too fast. He died instantly. Or so they tell me." She didn't say anything for a couple minutes. Annie could hardly breathe. Then Olivia went on, very softly, "And ever since then, my mom and dad haven't been the same. I think that they are trying to stay together for my sake, but I'm not sure they're going to make it. I think my dad might be having an affair. I don't know for sure. My mom tries to be brave, but she is just so sad."

Olivia lay flat on her back, not even moving a muscle. But in the dark, Annie could see tears trailing down her cheeks. Tears like silver rain. She reached over and hugged Olivia. She couldn't really think of anything to say. Olivia hugged her back gratefully.

"So, you see," Olivia said, "when Mrs. Murphy was talking about the sacred hurt, I felt like she was talking right to me. I know that you felt like she was talking right to you, Annie, but she was talking to me too."

Annie hugged her tighter. "I am so sorry. I didn't know. You're right. I felt

like she was talking right to me." She lay
back down, flat on her back, staring up at
the ceiling. Olivia was doing the same
thing. Annie went on, "But a weird thing
happened to me as she was talking. I looked
around the room, and I saw several kids
nodding quietly as they listened to her. I
had the thought that maybe there were a lot
of them that had already experienced a
sacred hurt. But I just didn't know that one
of them was you. I'm so sorry."

"Oh, that's all right," Olivia said.
"Not many people do. I don't really talk
about it. But as she gave her lecture that
day, I started to realize that I needed to think
about the way I have been handling this
whole thing. I might not be allowing myself
to heal. I'm going to think about it.
Anyhow, I feel a little bit better having told
you tonight. Whatever sense that makes.
Goodnight, Annie. Thanks for letting me
spend the night." She hugged Annie tightly.

Annie hugged her back.
"Goodnight, Olivia. Thanks for telling me.
Somehow, it makes me feel better that you
did. I don't know why. But it does."

"Interesting, isn't it. The way our
minds work," Olivia whispered into the
night.

"And our hearts," Annie whispered
back.

Chapter 19

On Monday, Mrs. Murphy talked about the
first twenty pages of *The Old Man and the
Sea*, and Annie was pleased that she seemed
to lay stress on two things she had already
noticed herself—Santiago's hopeful spirit,
and the dreams of lions. In fact, Mrs.
Murphy had everybody underline or
highlight the very passages that Annie had
already marked for herself. True, she had
the added advantage of following in her
mom's footsteps across the pages, but Annie
had a feeling that she would have marked
them anyway, all on her own. Mrs. Murphy
added that, right from the beginning,
Hemingway was helping us to see that
Santiago, although he had clearly suffered
many sorrows, had a great heart. A boy
named Greg, who was sitting next to Olivia,
raised his hand to ask a question. Annie
noticed how well behaved the class was
recently. Now that everyone was more used
to Mrs. Murphy's style of teaching, she
never had to raise her voice.

In fact, it felt like a big change had
swept through the room after her talk about
the sacred hurt. Greg said, "What should we
make of those dreams of the lions, Mrs.
Murphy? I also noticed that it said that the
old man never dreamed of his wife anymore.
Or of great fish or great battles or even of
women. Only of lions. I am not sure what

to make of that." There were several quiet whispers from the other students, indicating that they too were curious about the lions.

"Well," said Mrs. Murphy, "you have correctly identified a very important question for us as scholars. What are we to make of the recurrent dreams of the lions? We are going to have to watch this image because it repeats often throughout the novel. In fact, when all is said and done, we will still be talking about the lions." She let that sink in for a minute. Then, she said, "In studying great literature, you have to consider yourself sort of like a judge, hearing testimony from conflicting witnesses. It's too early in your reading of this novel for you to render any judgments yet. You need to read the whole thing, give yourself time to think about it, and then figure out what you believe. But—I'll tell you the truth. Part of what makes a very scholarly mind is learning how to ask the right questions. And you have just done that."

She smiled at Greg, and he smiled back. Annie was thinking about what she had just heard. In both the subject of sacred hurts and figuring out what a piece of literature was all about, Mrs. Murphy seemed to be cautioning patience. Not rushing to judgment. Annie realized that this is a very difficult thing to do, but she thought it sounded like a good idea. Mrs.

Murphy told them to read the next twenty pages for homework tonight. Annie flipped to the end of the book and realized that it was only about 125 pages long, so, at this rate, they would be finishing it pretty quickly. She liked the character of Santiago, and she liked the boy too. She actually found herself looking forward to the reading tonight, after cross-country practice.

At practice that afternoon, Annie found out that she would be running for time in Thursday's meet. The coach pulled her aside right at the beginning of practice. It was late September now, and October would arrive tomorrow. There was a definite nip in the air as the runners lined up on the track. While they were all milling around, Mr. Place called her over.

"Annie, you had the sixth best time for girls in the last practice, so you will be running for time in this week's meet. I'm really impressed with your progress. Keep up the good work. We usually don't have freshmen whose times count. As you know, only the top six times count, but we think you could have one of them. We have a dual meet against Bentley High School. We're running here, on our home track, and we think you can bring in a really good time for us. So, go out there and have a good, solid run this afternoon, and we will see what happens on Thursday," he looked down at his clipboard and called everyone over. Annie's heart was thumping, but Mr. Place had clearly moved on to other concerns.

Then he addressed the whole team, saying, "Let's have a good run today. You know we have a big meet on Thursday. So, take it cool and don't overexert yourselves, but give us a good time. Notice that the weather is changing. So, stretch before you start your run. We don't want any pulled muscles. We will not be keeping times today. Just have a good run."

Everyone bent over and started their personal stretching routine. A boy named Tom, who was the junior class president came over and stood beside Annie. She didn't think anything of it until suddenly he spoke to her.

"Hey," he said. "I'm Tom Marino." He smiled at her.

"Hi," Annie answered. "I know who you are. Junior class president and cross-country star." It was true what she said. Everybody did know who he was. He had longish blonde hair that just curled over his collar, and a hunk of it that kept falling in his eyes. Annie had the feeling that he knew that he was hot, but he was, and so that was that.

"So, what's up, Tom?" She was surprised at the confidence she heard in her own voice. It sounded like she was flirting with Tom, and very confidently. She didn't feel confident at all, but she sounded like she did. She felt like she was playing a part in a movie. But, she was playing it well.

He smiled. "Well, I was wondering if you might like to go to Homecoming with me. It's in three weeks, but I thought I'd ask you now before somebody else did." Annie practically choked. That might be the last thing she ever expected him to say.

"You want to go to Homecoming with me?" she sputtered. "I'm sorry, but you're not teasing, are you? I mean, I'm just a freshman! I didn't think you even knew my name."

"Well, some of us 'older guys' pay careful attention to the freshmen girls. Sometimes, it's nice to take someone to the dance that doesn't know all the cliques and groups. Someone who approaches the event with an open mind—ready for new experiences." Annie considered the possibility that there was a double entendre lurking under his words, but his eyes were twinkling in the afternoon sun, and he seemed very nice.

"Well, I would be honored," she said.

"Then, how about the varsity football game this Friday? Seven?" He seemed very sure of himself.

Annie said, "That will be great. I'll be ready." Meanwhile, all the runners had finished their stretching and were taking off on the run.

"All right, then," said Tom. He smiled at her, patted her on the shoulder and said, "have a good run."

Annie stood there, grinning. Again, she felt like she had been branded. What was going on? How had the whole world suddenly changed? Why were boys suddenly noticing her? She was not prepared for all of these new feelings, and she desperately wished her mom were still alive so she could run some of these questions by her.

She thought about asking her dad, but when she tried to put the doubts into words, it all sounded stupid She decided to keep her thoughts to herself and just act like she knew what she was doing.

But, that night at dinner, she told him that she was running for time in the cross-country meet on Thursday. Then, she added that Tom Marino had asked her to go to a football game with him.

"That's great, Annie," her dad said, "I mean about the cross-country meet. That is just amazing that you have one of the top times and you're only a freshman. Must be those long legs of yours. But about Tom Marino. I don't know. I don't really know him because I only teach seniors and he is a junior. But he has the reputation of being just a little bit fast. If that's the right word these days. I know he's kind of a 'big man on campus,' if you know what I mean. I wonder if he might be a little too grown up for you." He was looking right at Annie, and she could see the worry and concern in his eyes.

"Dad," she said. "I'll be fine. There are hundreds of kids at the football game. You know that. Nothing can happen there. The truth is, he also asked me to Homecoming, and then he followed that up with an invitation to the football game this Friday night. I said yes to both, because I actually think it would be a good idea to get to know him before the Homecoming dance." She was trying to be calm and persuasive, but she knew that her dad was pretty good at reading between the lines.

Eddie and Sarah were oblivious to their conversation, both of them spooning in their macaroni and cheese as fast as they could. Her dad frowned, "Oh, Annie. I don't know about this. He is at least two years older than you. He runs with a completely different crowd. Can I ask around first, see what I can find out about him?"

Annie said, "Dad, that's so awkward and embarrassing. Of course, you'll do what you want, but I think I should go to the football game and see for myself what he's like. He is a cross-country runner too, you know. That's how he knows me."

Finishing his dinner, her dad said, "Well, all right. But, let's talk between now and Friday about defensive measures you might need to know when you're out on a date with a young man."

Annie giggled, "Dad, you make it sound like it's going to be hand to hand combat or something. Stop worrying so much."

Her dad said, "Listen, Annie. Sometimes, that's exactly what it is. So, I will say yes to this date for Friday, but with very strict rules and a very strict curfew. Home by eleven. No later, and no kidding."

Annie said, "Fine. But you're being silly." He shot her a warning look. "But I will tell him the rules," she conceded. She helped her dad clear the table and thought about the thrill of being picked up by a guy in a car and taken to a game. Or to a dance. Or anywhere. The whole world was changing.

Chapter 20

Tom picked her up about 6:30, and the game started at 7:00. She had on jeans and a sweater, because there was a distinct chill in the air. October was upon them. He came to the door to pick her up and introduced himself to her dad, handling himself very well. He had longish blonde hair that fell in his eyes, and he was always kind of pushing it back. And those eyes. A girl could get lost in those eyes. Deep pools of brown that sparkled like stones on the bottom of a river. He had on jeans and his varsity jacket, with stripes on the sleeves for his two years as a varsity runner so far. Her dad told him, in no uncertain terms, that she was to be home by eleven, and Tom said that would be no problem. Finally, she was in the car, buckling her seatbelt, away from her dad and the kids and everything that seemed, at that moment, to be holding her back. She could hardly contain her excitement.

Tom grinned at her. "Your dad's kind of strict with you, right?" Oddly enough, even though she agreed with him, she felt an impulse to defend her dad.

"Well," she said. "I'm the oldest. And he's trying to figure all of this out by himself, you know. Without a wife to guide him." She tried to laugh a little, to seem to make light of it.

Tom looked over at her with some alarm in his eyes. "Are your parents divorced?" He was driving carefully as they approached the school and hundreds of cars were jockeying for position to get into the parking lot. Annie suddenly felt incredibly awkward and wished she had not said anything about her mom and dad. But there was no escaping it now.

"No," she said. "My mom died two years ago from cancer. So, he's been trying to figure out a lot of stuff by himself. And teach full time, of course. He's pretty brave."

"Wow," said Tom. "That's heavy. No, I'm sorry. I didn't know. I guess I just haven't been paying attention. My parents are divorced, and I live with my mom. But I still see my dad a lot. Anyhow, I guess I just assumed that you were in a similar situation." He found a parking spot.

"Really, I would give anything to be in that situation," said Annie. "Divorce sounds so much less final that death." She looked over at him. "Sorry. I don't mean to underestimate how hard divorce is." She felt like she had just said something really stupid and insensitive.

"No worries," he said. "To tell you the truth, it's been all right for me. They did not get along, and the house is a lot quieter now. And my dad makes a lot of money and bought me this car, sort of to stay on my good side, even though I live with my mom. So, it kind of works out for me." They got out of the car and he locked the doors. "But, just between you and me, I sort of miss the times when we were all together. Back when it all worked." Then, suddenly, he seemed to realize that he had revealed something too personal and quickly dropped the subject.

Annie understood that she should not ask any further questions. He put his hand on her back to guide her toward the line to get into the game. She couldn't get used to being touched by a guy; it was still such a new sensation. But, she had to admit, she kind of liked it. As they got in line, he stood behind her, and Annie was aware of his closeness. Weird rockets were going off in her head. She was excited and just a little bit frightened. But definitely interested.

They got into the game and sought out the student section. There were hundreds of students already there, and Tom guided her up the bleachers to where a couple of his buddies were sitting.

One of them, a guy named Mike, grinned when they approached. "Hey, Tom," he said, with a smile that did not quite look friendly at all. "Robbing the cradle?"

Although Annie had not heard that term before, her mind was racing and she figured out very quickly that he was making a disparaging remark about how young she was. Compared, of course, to him—so wise and worldly, she thought sarcastically.

Tom ignored him and they sat down. The game had already started and the home team was winning. You could smell hot dogs and hot chocolate in the air. The marching band was playing, and the cheerleaders were gyrating on the field right below where they were sitting. The whole spectacle seemed kind of wonderful to Annie, who drank all the sights and sounds in eagerly. As she was sitting there watching the next play, Mike leaned down and whispered something in her ear. At first, she didn't quite catch what he said, but she smelled liquor. Or at least, she thought she did. It surprised her. Mike was a runner too. Shouldn't he be keeping himself ready to compete? Also, the coach had said something about no drinking and no doing anything that could get you in trouble in school. She turned around and said, "I'm sorry. I didn't catch what you said."

Mike laughed and said, "Probably better that way. Sorry. I'll be on my best behavior. You look good tonight, Annie. All grown up." Annie turned around to look at him quickly, not sure what to make of his remark, or his tone.

She didn't know if he was messing with her or just being nice. She could feel herself blushing. She turned around and said nothing, instead concentrating on the game. Oddly enough, Tom either had not noticed or did not care. She wasn't sure which one was the best description. She couldn't think of anything clever to say, so she decided to just ignore the whole thing.

Meanwhile, the teams were bashing each other on the field of combat. She thought about her sport—cross-country—compared to football and realized that there wasn't much of a comparison. Nobody was trying to hit her while she ran on the path. She felt her admiration for the football players increase. They were either very brave, or crazy. Or maybe a little bit of both. After the game, Tom took her straight home, obedient to the curfew. On the porch, just before he went in, he kissed her on the mouth. She wasn't ready for it, and it really caught her off guard. He seemed to notice her reaction, and he kissed her again, this time gently on the cheek. He said, "I had fun tonight, Annie." And then he was gone.

Annie stood there with her head spinning. What was going on? She had never really been kissed by a boy. But she had now, and she knew it. Suddenly, the word "kiss" did not mean what it used to mean. Not at all. She opened the door and went into her house, preparing to tell her dad about the game. Just the game. She wondered what her mom would have to say about Tom and his kiss. She could almost guess. Almost.

Chapter 21

On Monday, the whole school was buzzing with gossip. There was an audible hum in the hallways when Annie walked in. Kids were clustered in groups around their classroom doors, whispering feverishly to each other, looking down or away when teachers walked by. Annie had no idea what was going on. But then, she was always the last one to know anything, or so it seemed. She walked into her homeroom, and the same buzz was going on. Olivia hurried over to her, and her face looked almost pale.

"Annie," she said. "Did you hear what happened?" Annie shook her head no, and the words tumbled out of Olivia, as if she was powerless to stop them. This was kind of interesting, because Olivia wasn't really the kind of girl to engage in idle gossip. And somehow, that did not seem to be what she was doing now. She was genuinely frightened. "You know that girl that sits in the last desk in the first row in our English class? She's kind of pretty? Blonde hair, long ponytail, big blue eyes? Very quiet?" Annie turned and looked at the empty desk, as if that could call the girl to mind. Oddly enough, it did. She had noticed her many times, just because she was very pretty. But they hadn't really spoken to each other.

She turned back to Olivia and nodded, "Yes. I know who you mean, but I don't really know her."

Olivia said, "I don't think anybody feels like they know her right now. Her name is Zoe. Anyhow, this weekend, she tried to commit suicide. She took a whole bottle of sleeping pills that she took from her mom's bedside table. And just went to sleep. She would have died, but her mom came in to check on her and tried to talk to her, and nothing. She called 911, and they came and got her and pumped her stomach. She's in the hospital right now."

Annie sat down hard in her desk. She felt like she couldn't even stand up right now. Why would anyone do that? Her head was spinning. Olivia gave her a quick hug and went to her own desk, getting ready for the first bell to ring. The bell rang and the teacher called the class to order.

Annie felt a weird buzzing in her head. She couldn't seem to focus on anything that was being said from the front of the room, and she could hear the other kids all whispering in quiet, shocked voices. It's not like Annie knew Zoe all that well, but the truth is, she had kind of admired her from a distance. She seemed like a good student, and she was very pretty. All the boys noticed her, with her long blonde ponytail, and big blue eyes. Who wouldn't? It seemed like she had some good girl friends. So, what could have gone so wrong? How in the world did it all seem so hopeless that she just wanted to go to sleep forever?

Annie thought back to the last days she had with her mom, when she had clung to life, even though every conscious moment was filled with pain. She had fought so hard to hang on, and yet Zoe just wanted to lay down and die. Annie felt tears pricking at the sides of her eyes, and a roaring in her head. The bell rang, and all the students moved to their desks, but each person seemed to be moving in a daze. Annie noticed that a couple of the girls were quietly crying, tears sliding down their cheeks. There was a weird quiet in the classroom, the whispering buzz gone now.

Mrs. Murphy called the class to attention. She asked that everyone take a quiet moment, all to themselves, and send a good thought or prayer to Zoe, hoping that the good doctors who have her in their care can bring her back to them quickly. Then she said, "I know that this has been a terrible thing for all of you to experience and hear. I know that some of you are good friends with Zoe, and you may know much more about what has brought her to this moment in her life than I do. But I know this about Zoe. She is a very good student in this class, a careful and diligent scholar. I think we can honor her best by pushing on with our

155

studies. You might make a mental note of where we are today, because Zoe is going to want someone to help her catch up when she gets back. And that might be a real opportunity for you to show Zoe that you care very much about her. And that might be exactly what she needs to hear."

It was such an interesting thing to say. Instead of dwelling on the hurt, with no plan of action, you should acknowledge the hurt and then try to move on. Annie was fascinated by the approach, and further fascinated when everyone pulled out their copies of *The Old Man and the Sea*, opening them to the second section, as directed.

Mrs. Murphy said, "We had a good discussion the other day about the idea of a sacred hurt. Some of you have already experienced that, and the idea just got a lot more real for many of you. Let's pick up Santiago's story where it really begins. The old man has had 85 days of bad luck, returning after a day on the sea with nothing to show for his efforts. The parents of the young boy who loves him have forced their son to abandon Santiago, believing that the old man's luck has simply run out. They need food on their table, and they make their son go to work with more profitable, younger men on other fishing boats. In spite of this, Santiago persists in believing that his luck is about to change, and so, on the eighty-fifth day of his unlucky streak, he sets out alone, sailing far beyond the island's shallow coastal waters, entering the Gulf Stream. He baits his lines and drops them into the water. At about noon, everything changes, and all at once. Would anyone like to talk about that moment in the story?"

A boy sitting at the back of the class whose name was Paul Miller put his hand up. Mrs. Murphy nodded at him. "Go ahead, Paul," she said.

"Well," Paul said, "at about noon, the old man hooks a really big fish. He thinks it's a marlin. The old man can't pull the fish in, and pretty soon, the big fish starts to pull the old man out to sea."

"That's right," said Mrs. Murphy. "Then what happens?" She nodded for Paul to continue, and he seemed ready to do so. Annie turned around in her desk so she could see him better. His voice was actually kind of soft. This was the first time she had ever heard him speak. He had soft brown hair and a very pale complexion. He was thin, but had a look of quiet strength about him.

He looked down at the top of his desk, cleared his throat, and seemed to gather himself to go on, saying, "Well, er…that begins two whole days and nights of torture. The fish pulls the boat all day and all night, and the whole day and night the next day too. The old man has wrapped the fishing line around his shoulders to keep the line from snapping, so he is essentially tied to the fish himself. He goes through hell. Oops, sorry."

Paul just seemed to run out of air, all of a sudden. It was like he couldn't bring himself to go on. Annie wondered about that, and Mrs. Murphy seemed to sense it too. She nodded her approval at what Paul had said and asked if anyone would like to add anything to that.

A girl who sat next to Paul put her hand up. Her name was Tiffany. She was a little bit heavy, but with beautiful dark hair. And very quiet, ordinarily. But she seemed compelled to talk right now. Mrs. Murphy nodded to her, asking her what she would like to add. Tiffany said, "I think that at this point in the story, I really started to feel sorry for him. Suddenly, he struck me as a very old man. I mean—I knew all along that he was old. But now, somehow, he seemed *very* old. In way over his head. He kept saying to himself how much he missed the boy, and trying to pray and forgetting the words. And talking to the fish, the great fish that he had caught."

"Very good," said Mrs. Murphy. "And did you notice his attitude toward the fish starting to change? And if so, how would you describe that change?"

Tiffany's eyes lit up. "Yes, I did. At first, he seemed to think of the fish as the enemy. Or a prize he could win. But about this time in the story, the fish became kind of a companion, or a worthy adversary." She wasn't sure if she had gone too far, but Mrs. Murphy smiled at her and nodded, encouraging her.

"Well done, Tiffany," Mrs. Murphy said. "You have hit on a very important idea right there. Go on." She smiled at Tiffany, who seemed to grow a little more confident about what she wanted to say.

Tiffany smiled slightly and continued, "It almost seemed like he started to feel sorry for having caught the fish. Is that stupid?"

Mrs. Murphy reassured her, saying, "Not at all. I think you are absolutely right. Can anyone find a passage that supports what Tiffany is saying?"

A girl named Jessica, who sat up front, put her hand up and said that the old man was hoping that the fish did not know just how powerful he really was, but he also said, 'I'll kill him though…in all his greatness and his glory.'

"Very good," Mrs. Murphy agreed, asking her to give the page number so that everyone could mark the passage in their books. "And, about this time, the old man starts to worry about a new problem, a problem that becomes very real, very quickly. Can anyone tell me what that is?"

Several hands went up, but the bell rang, and Mrs. Murphy quickly said that they would continue tomorrow and that everyone should finish reading the book tonight. She further reminded them to keep Zoe in their thoughts, hoping that if they all did that, she would feel their strength flowing into her.

The rest of the day went by in a blur, with nothing living up to the thoughts and feelings she had experienced in her English class that morning. After school, Annie swung by her dad's room to tell him that she had cross country practice after school and that she had a chance to maybe run for points in the district match this Thursday. He wished her well and told her to be careful. He seemed to be very proud of her, and Annie felt happy that she had made him so proud.

When she stepped outside the school, after slipping into her running clothes in the locker room, she was surprised by the change in the weather. The wind bit sharply, and the cold stung her eyes. She headed out to the track, and saw the other runners filing out all around her. They gathered at the entrance to the trail, many of the runners bouncing up and down to try to stay warm. The coach reminded everyone to stretch, and he said he would shoot a starter pistol to start the run today so that they could get used to the sound of it. Annie nodded and thought to herself that he was really trying to get them ready for the race on Thursday. She quickly stretched and got ready. He fired the starting pistol, and it did startle her, but suddenly everyone was off running.

Annie started out at what she felt was a brisk pace, but not too fast. She felt many runners go right past her, moving out quickly, but she wanted to run within herself and have enough left for a strong finish. Soon, the trail got rougher, the gravel cold and sharp in the wintry temperatures. The trees had mostly been stripped of their leaves by now. Only the old, scraggly oak trees hung on to the last, forlorn brown leaves. They rustled overhead, but it did not sound like hands clapping to Annie. Not like the poplar leaves of summer. It sounded more like an angry whisper, with no hint of summer or laughter anywhere at all.

Annie chugged along, glancing up quickly at the trees overhead. She thought to herself that now that the winter was almost here, the trees were revealing their architecture. It seemed to her as if the branches were the bones of the tree, lit up against the x-ray gray of the afternoon sky. Annie shivered a little, in spite of the fact that she was running, feeling the winter upon her once again. Summer seemed like a long time ago—a distant memory.

All of a sudden, the toe of her running shoe caught on a root that was swollen up in the pathway. Annie felt her ankle turn out in a sickening crunch as she stumbled. She was launched into a full-out airborne sprawl, skidding to a stop in the trail. Unfortunately, there must have several runners right behind her, and they tripped over her, two of them also going down. They quickly jumped back up though, made sure that she was all right, and then got back into the run. Annie had a face full of dirt and gravel and a throbbing pain in her right ankle. She tried to stand up and crumpled right back down. One of the senior captains got her cell phone out and called the coach. She told Annie to sit down and stay down until the coach got there.

Annie kind of half dragged herself off the trail and out of the other runners' way. They called out to her as they ran by, asking if she needed help and if someone had called the coach. She waved them on and sat there, her back against an old oak tree, feeling stupid and hurt. Her ankle was really throbbing now. She couldn't put any weight on it at all.

Within four minutes, her coach and the athletic trainer were there, riding up to her in a golf cart. He and the trainer got her into the golf cart and gave her a ride back to the school. There, the trainer put a quick splint on her ankle and called her dad, who luckily was still at school. He came over immediately in the car, and using some borrowed crutches, Annie hobbled out to the car, thanking the trainer and apologizing to everyone for having caused so much trouble.

She was embarrassed to find tears in the corners of her eyes. Her dad told her over and over again not to worry. They swung by Eddie and Sarah's school and picked them up. Eddie was fascinated with Annie's crutches and could hardly wait to try them. Her dad called Mrs. Murphy on his phone and asked if she could keep an eye on Eddie and Sarah while they went to the hospital. She said that her schedule was wide open and asked if he could bring the kids to her at school. She was still there. He said sure and ran them in to her, and then he and Annie headed off to the hospital.

By now, Annie's ankle was absolutely throbbing. It felt to her like she could feel her heartbeat in her ankle. In a daze of pain, she dimly wondered if there was any significance to her dad asking Mrs. Murphy to watch the kids. In some part of her brain, she registered that this was just a little bit unexpected. But she was too wrapped up in her throbbing ankle to consider it too deeply. She wondered if Zoe was in this hospital, all hooked up to wires and tubes, and if she was feeling any better. She asked her dad if he could find out if Zoe was anywhere around.

He went to the nurse's station and asked if they could tell him where she was, although he clearly did not want to miss the doctor coming to look at Annie. He found out that Zoe was on the third floor, and Annie asked if they could see her before they went home. He hesitated for a couple of minutes and then said that he would look into it after they got the results from her x-ray. And then they did. It was a fracture. Not a horrible one, but one that would require a cast for a few weeks. Annie's heart sank. It just didn't seem fair.

Her dad left the room where she was waiting for a doctor to come and put a cast on her foot and came back twenty minutes later, saying that they could see Zoe if she still wanted to. The doctor asked Annie what color of cast she wanted, and oddly enough, that was the first time she really understood what that meant. A cast. On her leg. In a daze, she told him blue, and she didn't even know why she had chosen that color. When he was done putting the cast on, she looked down at her leg, now encased in a horrible Smurf blue cast. She wondered what in the world she had been thinking. It was *really* blue. She fought back tears, and not just from pain. Her dad said that he had received permission for them to have a quick visit with Zoe. She thanked the doctor, grabbed her crutches, and hobbled into the elevator to go up to the third floor.

She moved very slowly and awkwardly on the crutches. Her dad walked behind her, letting her set the pace, saying that everything would be all right. Telling her not to feel bad, and to hang in there. When they got to Zoe's room, Annie peeked in timidly. She hardly recognized her. Zoe was hooked up to tubes and wires, and she looked so pale. And thin. Her hair was pulled back from her face into a high ponytail, and it looked kind of tight and uncomfortable. Zoe smiled, sadly, and said, "Hey. What did you do to yourself?"

Annie shuffled into a chair beside Zoe's bed and said, trying to smile, "I fell down on the cross-country trail, right before a big district meet." Annie suddenly noticed that Zoe's mom was standing in the back corner of the room. She looked terrible. Annie's dad seemed to notice at the very same moment. He asked her if he could buy her a cup of coffee, to give the girls some time alone. She seemed almost desperately grateful for the excuse to escape her vigil, even if only for a few moments. Annie's dad escorted her out of the room gently, talking quietly about the girls and Annie's fall today.

Annie looked at Zoe and said, "I don't want to bother you. I know you must still feel pretty sick. I just wanted to tell you that everybody at school is really worried about you. And Mrs. Murphy said that you're a really good student in English class, and so am I. And we started that new unit on *The Old Man and the Sea*. And I take really good notes. I almost write down everything she says. And I wanted to let you know that you could borrow my book and that I would be glad to help you when you get back. If you want." Now that she had delivered the speech, it seemed sort of stupid. After all, a couple of days ago, Zoe did not think life was worth living anymore, and here was Annie, talking about what was going on in English class. Stupid, stupid, stupid. She could feel herself blushing, right down to her roots. But instead of getting angry or sad, Zoe actually smiled. Sort of a sad little smile, but a smile just the same.

"That would be really great," she said softly. "I think I'll get out of here tomorrow, and I should be returning to school next week." She swallowed hard, wincing as though her throat were sore. "I can't even begin to tell you how much I am dreading that. Going back to school. Everyone looking at me like I'm some kind of freak." She tried to laugh, but couldn't quite pull it off.

Annie sat quietly for a minute, putting herself in Zoe's shoes. She could understand how she might think that would happen. But she kept thinking about what she had been learning in English class. She cleared her throat and said softly, "To tell you the truth, Zoe, I don't think you should worry about it at all. Mrs. Murphy gave this

166

lecture about a sacred hurt. In connection with the Hemingway novel, and she was explaining that almost everybody experiences a sacred hurt, sooner or later. And that means that something happens to you that is so bad that it really hurts, and it causes you to reevaluate everything. And some things that once seemed possible, no longer are. And you know it. And you kind of have to allow yourself to grieve for that loss of innocence. Allow yourself to hurt. Go down to the bottom. And then, swim back up to the surface, and keep swimming."

Annie felt herself blushing again. She wondered if she had gone too far, sounded too preachy. She dropped her gaze to her hands, which were resting in her lap. But she went on. The words came out of her, softly, but with some weird kind of power: "And, I was sitting there, thinking about my mom, and how much I missed her. And that I knew what a sacred hurt was. And I looked around the room, and I saw quite a few people with an eye-lock on Mrs. Murphy, quietly nodding as if they knew what she meant. That really made me think, and I decided something. I'm just going to keep on swimming." She looked up to see if she was annoying Zoe.

Instead of looking annoyed, Zoe smiled again, another sad little smile. "Like Dory in *Finding Nemo*?" she said.

167

Annie laughed. She said, "You know—I hadn't made that connection. But, you're right. Like *Finding Nemo*. Anyhow, I know it sounds silly, but—a lot of kids started talking about sacred hurts they've been through. And I realized something. You kind of think that you are the only one with problems, and the truth is, everybody in that room is hurting, one way or another. I didn't feel like anybody was making fun of you at all. I think you can come back without worrying about that. People might look at you a little differently, but it might just be because they know you've experienced a sacred hurt."

Zoe was quiet for a minute, and then she said, "Thanks a lot for coming by. You've cheered me up more than you know. And I really would appreciate help with the story. It sounds like something I'm going to like." Just then Zoe's mom and Annie's dad walked back in the room. They each held a paper cup of coffee, and Zoe's mom was smiling at something that Annie's dad had said. Annie had a quick moment of appreciation for her dad's gentle ways.

"Come on, Annie. Let's get out of their hair," her dad said. Zoe's mom thanked them for coming by, and Zoe added her thanks, too.

She smiled at Annie and said, "I'll see you next week. And thanks for the offer of help with English. I'm going to take you up on that." Annie said goodbye, hobbled up, grabbed her crutches and limped out to the car.

The wind had a mean, cold edge to it, and Annie could feel November about to make her presence felt. She thanked her dad for helping her to see Zoe, and she told him that she thought it was a good thing they had dropped by. He seemed to be very pleased at what she said about Zoe wanting her help with English class.

When they got home, her dad thanked Mrs. Murphy for helping out with Eddie and Sarah. She had fed them dinner, and they were watching cartoons. Mrs. Murphy said to Annie, "So, what's the verdict? How long do you have to have that lovely thing on?" Her dad told her that it might be a month. That it was only a stress fracture, but that it was right on the border of a full-fledged fracture. Mrs. Murphy smiled at Annie and said, "So I guess you're going to Homecoming with that on. That is lousy luck. I'm so sorry."

It was actually the first time that Annie had realized that. She had not even thought about Homecoming at all. "Oh, man," she said. "You're right. Wow. That is just horrible." She tried to picture what kind of dress could go with a big, blue hulking cast. No kind of dress. Then, she remembered what she wanted to tell her teacher. "But, I wanted to tell you that we

169

went by Zoe's room in the hospital, and I told her what you said about sacred hurts, and it seemed to help her a lot."

Mrs. Murphy smiled gently. "Oh Annie, I am so glad to hear that." She gathered her coat and her briefcase up. "And now, I must say goodnight. I have to get home and grade some papers." She hugged Annie's dad briefly and left. Her dad stood at the front door and watched her drive away, waving goodbye.

Then, he gave Annie a pill to help with the pain and a bowl of chicken noodle soup. Annie sort of hopped over to the couch and watched cartoons with Eddie and Sarah. She suddenly was absolutely exhausted. And she felt like pretending, at least for a little while, that she was six years old again.

Chapter 22

Her father had taken her shopping for a dress for Homecoming. They didn't have anyone to watch Eddie and Sarah, so they had had to drag them along. The whole trip was a complete disaster. Annie found it exhausting to traipse through the stores on her crutches. Some guy in "Customer Service" offered them a wheelchair, and Annie was so exhausted that she thought it might actually be better, even if it was embarrassing. The only problem was that Sarah said she was too tired to walk anymore and made Annie let her sit on her lap. They looked like such a spectacle, roaring around the mall, with Eddie zooming in and out of the displays and wanting only to go to a video game store. They finally ended up with a dark blue slip dress that didn't clash too horribly with the stupid blue cast she had chosen.

Annie found herself wishing that she had never agreed to go to the dance; she certainly couldn't *dance* at the dance! Unless clomping around like some weird kind of Frankenstein was acceptable. Plus, ever since she had broken her leg and missed the district meet, Tom Marino had seemed kind of cold to her. Like he didn't really want to go with her at all anymore, but had to since he had invited her in a moment of madness. Or pity. Annie could not shake the persistent bad feeling that seemed to surround the whole thing when she thought about it. On the night of the dance, Olivia came over to do Annie's makeup since she herself was not going to the dance. Olivia seemed to understand a little bit of Annie's hesitation about the night, but she kept trying to cheer her up as she did her hair and eyes. Annie had the impression that Olivia was trying to think of all the ways that this night might turn out all right.

Olivia said, "Annie, come on! This is so cool. You're just a freshman, and

171

you're going to the Homecoming Dance with a junior. And not just any junior. Tom Marino! He's so hot, a big man on campus, and he is *your* date! Think of that! And put a smile on your face. You look much prettier when you're smiling!" She smiled encouragingly at Annie, inviting her to smile back.

Annie grimaced at herself in the mirror. Olivia bent double, laughing. "Tell me that you do *not* think that is a smile. That's horrible. All right. Don't smile right now. I'm starting to work on your eyes, and smiling will not help." Olivia was like an artist, wielding brushes and colors. She told Annie to sit very still.

Annie said, "I just have this terrible feeling that he asked me to the dance on the spur of the moment. I don't really know him at all, and I don't hang with his crowd. I'm not cool enough for him. Also, I think that he's much more 'experienced' than I am. And that scares me, too." She felt a little silly saying this, but she was starting to feel safe around Olivia, and it was so nice to have someone to confide in.

Olivia said, "You mean sex?" Annie nodded. "Well," said Olivia. "I think you are probably right about that. Tom Marino could get any girl he wants. But just remember what you've always been told: You are the boss. Just say no if you're uncomfortable. If it comes to that." She finished her work on Annie's eyes and twirled Annie's chair around so she could see the results. Annie had to admit that Olivia knew what she was doing. Her hair and her eyes had never looked so good, but she also looked a little bit terrified. Or too grown up. Not quite herself. Or something.

She thanked Olivia for doing such a wonderful job and hobbled into the bathroom to get the last little bit of pee out before Tom came to the door. Then, she carefully crutched her way downstairs, where her dad was waiting for her in the kitchen. When she rounded the corner, he gave a low whistle of appreciation.

"Honey," he said. "You look just beautiful. You really do. But you look awfully grown up all of a sudden. I'm not sure I like it at all." He smiled at her, hugged her carefully, and then he thanked Olivia for all of her help.

Just then, the doorbell rang, and Tom Marino was waiting on the porch, with a blue and white corsage in a cellophane box in his hands. Tom was very polite to her father and to Eddie and Sarah, who were there to see Annie's "boyfriend"—even though she had told them, over and over, that he was *not* her boyfriend, not even close. Then, suddenly, her dad draped a shawl over her shoulders. It caught Annie off guard, because she had not been planning on wearing anything over her dress. The shawl was beautiful—creamy white silk with blue flowers on it. It really wasn't warm at all, but it definitely added a layer of elegance to her dress. And in her stupid cast and crutches, Annie felt anything but elegant. She looked up at her dad, "Dad, where did this come from? It's beautiful." He smiled at her and said, his voice gruff, "It was your mom's. I knew, once you picked out that dress, that it would be beautiful with it. I wanted to surprise you." He was a little choked up, Annie could tell.

Olivia exclaimed, "You look beautiful, Annie." She gave Annie a quick hug and said that Pierre was there to pick her up and take her home. She made Annie promise to text her and tell her everything when she got home, and then she gave Annie a quick hug and ran out the door to the big black car that was there waiting for her.

Suddenly, Annie realized that it was time to go, and she felt a little choked up herself, gently touching her mom's beautiful shawl. Her dad seemed to realize that all of a sudden, and he cheerfully changed the subject. "Now, just a reminder, Tom. Annie is just fifteen. Next week, actually. That means she still has a curfew, and I expect you to observe it. She is to be home here by midnight. I know that the dance ends at 10:30, so that should be workable.

Understood?" He gave Tom a meaningful look.

"Understood, sir. I will take good care of Annie. Goodnight, everybody," Tom said, and placing his hand lightly on the small of her back, he escorted her, rather firmly, out to his car. He helped her into the front seat and placed her crutches carefully in the back. He had borrowed his dad's car for the night, and it was a beauty. A black Mercedes CLS 63 AMG.

Annie knew enough about cars to know that this one was a beast. When she was a little girl, her dad had taught her all about all the cars he wished he owned. When they drove down the street, he would say something like, "Now that is a Corvette. It has 454 horsepower," and on and on. So, Annie learned to recognize cars and pay attention to details, and for some reason, she had kept her interest in them. Therefore, she knew that she was getting into a very expensive car, and it was a thrill. Tom pulled out of her subdivision very sedately, but as soon as they were out of sight of Annie's house, he floored it. The car jumped forward like a tiger lunging at prey. Annie was thrilled, and just a little bit scared. The roar of the engine, the glamorous black interior, the music on the stereo, the smell of his cologne—it all worked together to almost overwhelm her senses. The ride to the convention center, where the dance was being held, was just too short. Annie would have been content to ride around in this black beast for an hour or so. But Tom had other plans.

He dropped her at the door and told her to wait while he parked the car. He said he would only be a minute. Annie stood, just outside the convention center double doors, leaning on her crutches, watching handsome couples entering the dance arm in arm. All of the girls were in very high heels. Some of them looked like they could hardly stand. Annie looked down at her toes, hanging out of her blue cast, and her ballet flat on her other foot. She felt hopelessly uncool.

She was, however, gratified to see that sometimes a whole big bunch of girls arrived, or a bunch of boys—obviously coming without real dates, just to make the scene. But there were also couples who looked like real couples, clinging to each other. Annie wondered if some of them had been drinking. It kind of looked like it. Some of the dresses were almost scandalous, as far as Annie was concerned. She saw almost bare breasts, just barely restrained by scraps of glittery fabric. She saw skirt lengths that amazed her. How could they even sit down in that dress, she thought to herself. She stood there in her very blue dress with her very blue cast and felt kind of out of her league. She found herself wishing that she were home, or spending the night at Olivia's, laughing and looking at social media posts together. Or at an old movie. She even thought it might be more fun to be home with her dad and the little kids, having popcorn and hot chocolate.

Suddenly, Tom was there, his keys jingling in his hands as he strutted up. He grinned at Annie, "Come on, Hop-along. Let's get you to a table." Annie did not think she liked being called Hop-along, but she let it slide. She grabbed her crutches and started hobbling in, him walking just slightly behind her. Once again, his hand was on the small of her back, but this time, he let it drift up under her mother's shawl. His hand on her bare skin sent shock waves through her whole body. She felt herself tremble, and she knew that he had felt it too. He got her inside the ballroom and over to the table that was reserved for them.

She was sitting with four other couples, all juniors, all Tom's friends. The girls looked at Annie with slightly condescending glances—the kind of smiles that are sugary sweet but feel insincere. Annie felt like an outsider. All the girls were beautiful and very sophisticated, or at least they looked like it. And all of them were in very, very sexy dresses. All four of the girls were wearing black dresses, very skimpy, and Annie wondered if she had maybe missed a memo establishing the dress code for the evening. Tom introduced everyone very quickly, Tracy, Tiffany, Eva, and Stephanie. He did it so quickly that Annie could not keep them straight. Besides that, they were all blonde, slim, and beautifully made up. Even Annie's dark hair seemed like it was against the rules tonight.

The DJ was playing music so loudly that conversation was almost impossible, but Annie found herself feeling grateful anyway. Tracy or Tiffany said that the staff had just put the dinner out so everyone got up to go make their plates at the buffet line. Tom told Annie that he would get her plate and that she should just sit tight. Annie was actually very thankful, because she had no idea how she could juggle crutches and a plate in a buffet line.

All the other people got up from the table, and Annie was left sitting there all alone. She felt terribly out of place. She reached in her small black purse and grabbed her phone, just to have something to do. No Service. This whole convention center must be a big block of lead. She put her phone away, looked up, and suddenly, Dylan was there. "Where did you come from?" Annie blurted out. It is not what she meant to say, and she wished she had not said it quite like that. But, anyhow, that's what came out. She realized how awkward it sounded and felt stupid. She could feel herself blushing, but it was probably too dark for him to notice.

Dylan grinned at her, "Glad to see you, too. I was sitting over there," he pointed at a table in the distance. "And I saw you sitting here all alone. Thought I would come over and keep you company. Our table hasn't been called yet. I think it's some sort of hierarchy, and you are sitting with some big shot juniors. Whereas I am sitting with a table full of freshmen. So, here I am. For a couple minutes. How's your leg?" He knelt in front of her, not wanting to sit at a table where he didn't really belong. Or so it seemed to Annie. And clearly, not intending to stay very long, either. He seemed to have perched there, just for a minute.

Annie shook her head, "Lousy. I guess it's just what they call a stress fracture, but it's right on the borderline of being a real fracture. Anyhow, my season is over. And it hurts. And I have this stupid cast on, and it itches. And I don't like my dress. And this is my mother's shawl, and that's making me a little sad, and I don't know anyone at this table, and all the girls are looking at me as if I had two heads, and…" Suddenly, there were tears in her eyes, and she could not believe that she had said all that. It just tumbled out, and then she hiccupped a big sob, choking back tears, and she felt so incredibly stupid. She suddenly worried that all of Olivia's beautiful eye makeup would be ruined. She dabbed carefully at her eyes with a table napkin, sniffling.

Suddenly, Dylan halfway stood up and put his arms around her. Annie didn't know which she was more surprised at—her own outburst or his response. Aware of the awkwardness of the situation, she couldn't seem to stop herself, and she cried on his shoulder. She cried softly, realizing that she had no idea that this was going to happen, and she could not seem to stop the tears. He just held her, and he did not say a word. She pulled herself together, hoping that no one else had noticed. Maybe, it just looked like they were hugging for a minute. Maybe.

He smelled good. She felt the shoulder of his jacket getting wet from her tears, and when sanity returned, she pulled back quickly, feeling weird and stupid and kind of horrified at what she had just done.

"I am so sorry," she gulped. "I don't know what got into me. That is just so damn awkward. Please forgive me. I can't believe I just said damn. I don't know what just happened." She was babbling, and she knew it. Could this get any worse?

"Well," he said softly. "I think you just sort of told the truth, as much to yourself as to me. If I had to guess, I would say that you have been holding yourself together for a very long time, trying really hard to be brave and cool. And you just sort of got overwhelmed." Annie looked at him, shocked at how perceptive he seemed to be. She was speechless, and maybe that was a good thing. Then, she gathered herself, remembering her good manners.

"I got the shoulder of your jacket all wet, and I am so sorry. I feel like an idiot," Annie said, wiping her nose and eyes with her mom's shawl.

"Don't be ridiculous," Dylan said. "I'm just glad I was here. But look, here comes your date. I'll check on you later. By the way, you look beautiful in that blue dress. Anyone can wear a black skimpy dress and look good. You did something entirely different, and you rock it."

He got up quickly, nodded to Tom and the other people from the table, and left. All of these juniors seemed to know who he was. Again, Annie registered a moment of surprise about Dylan. He seemed like a jerk sometimes, but then sometimes, he didn't.

Tom said, "What was all that about?" His voice registered some level of irritation.

Annie said, "Nothing. Nothing at all. Thanks for fixing my plate." She accepted the dinner plate from Tom and waited for everyone to sit. When they were all seated, she started to eat her dinner. There was some chicken and some pasta, a little bit of salad, and a dinner roll. Annie started to eat gratefully. She realized that she hadn't had anything to eat since breakfast. As she ate her dinner, the girls at the table started to talking, and their conversations swirled around her, but did not really include her. She noticed that none of the girls seemed to be eating at all—just sort of picking at the food on their plates, and looking around the room. It seemed like they were afraid they were going to miss something. The guys at the table—Mike from the football game, Jim, Preston from the pool party, and Max something—all seemed older to Annie. She felt like she was some sort of mistake at the table. Like that old Sesame Street game—which of these things does not belong.

Anyhow, there was no need for her to try to participate in the conversation. It galloped over her head, and all around her, including Tom, but somehow not including her. Then, suddenly, everyone was done eating and ready to dance. The music was loud and fast, and Annie knew that there was nothing she could do to that. One of the girls—maybe Tiffany—asked Tom if he would dance with her.

Tom turned to Annie and said, "Do you mind?" Annie could tell that he was anxious to get out on the dance floor with this girl Tiffany.

Annie smiled and said, "No, of course not. You go dance."

Tom nodded and gave her a quick kiss on the cheek. "All right, then. I'll be right back. There's a little flask under my chair if you would like to drop a little rum in your Coke. See you in a little bit."

Suddenly, the table was empty. Annie didn't know what shocked her more, the cavalier way Tom left her alone, the casual offer of alcohol, the music, the dresses. It was all just too much. She pasted a smile on her face and watched the couples out on the dance floor. If you could call it that. Her table was right next to the dance floor, so she could pretty much see everything that was going on.

Some of the couples looked like they were almost having sex out there, with girls lifting their skirts teasingly. She saw one girl's boob fall out of her dress, and she just laughed and tucked it back in. Annie couldn't believe how casual everyone seemed to be about stuff like that. She was wondering if they really felt that way or if they were just pretending.

However, Annie felt, once again, that a lot of people were trying to prove that they were the coolest, most dangerous people in the school. Or most outrageous. Annie watched from the sidelines for about thirty minutes, and she could see Tom in flashes. First one girl and then another grabbed him and danced with him. It seemed as if he had forgotten his promise to

183

be right back. She watched as he held one girl after another in his arms, pressing them close to his body, swirling them around, dipping them low. He was a really good dancer, and it looked like he had forgotten all about her. Annie felt tears welling up again. She reached under the table and grabbed her crutches and her purse, hobbling out into the lobby in search of the restroom.

The lights were much brighter out in the lobby, and Annie could look around and see the layout of the convention center. All the teachers who were chaperoning the dance were out there, sitting at tables and eating their dinner. As Annie hobbled by, she saw her biology teacher, Miss Boransky, sitting with one of the history teachers. All the boys had a crush on her. She was young, and smart, and pretty—and she knew it. But tonight, she got up from her seat and came over to Annie.

"Hi, Annie," she said quickly. "Are you doing all right? I promised your dad that I would try to keep an eye out for you tonight. Are you having fun?"

Annie pulled herself together and smiled. "Just taking a little break is all," she said. "Do you know where the restroom is, by any chance?"

"Just over there," said Miss Boransky. "Do you need any help or anything?"

She looked hard at Annie, as if she were trying to assess the situation. It was suddenly very important to Annie to seem as if she was fine.

"Oh, no, I'm fine," she said quickly. "Have a good night," she added. Miss Boransky smiled and said, "I will as soon as I can get out of here. The dance is over at 10:30, but they start letting kids go at 10:00, so things will start to quiet down pretty quickly now."

Annie did not know this piece of information, but she was glad to have found that out. What it meant is that she only had to survive about another hour and then, she might be free. She hobbled into the ladies' room, found an empty stall, sat down on the toilet and peed. And then she started to cry again. It caught her completely unawares, the tears streaming down her cheeks. She tried to dry her eyes and hobbled out to wash her hands. Standing at the sinks in front of a huge, long mirror were several other girls. One of them was clearly drunk and ran into the handicap stall, throwing up violently. Two others were standing there, trying to help her, holding her hair back and talking softly to her.

Another girl's dress strap had broken, and she was crying because no one could find a safety pin to put her back together. As it was now, her right boob was fully exposed. Annie thought to herself that the dress was probably two sizes too small for the girl anyhow. Some other girl was crying and blubbering about her boyfriend "cheating" on her with "some slut."

Annie stood there, leaning on her crutches, fighting back tears, and feeling like she actually did fit in, for the first time that night. She let the tears fall down her cheeks, and someone handed her a Kleenex. Another girl got a small stool for Annie to sit on, and Annie plopped her butt down gratefully, setting her crutches on the floor. Oddly enough, she felt content to just sit here for the rest of the night, watching other girls cry and gossip. After a few minutes, the other girls seemed to include Annie in their conversations. Misery loves company, and all that.

Before she knew it, forty minutes had gone by, and Annie knew that she had to get back to the table. She said goodnight to her new friends and gathered up her crutches. She did a quick little bit of repair on her makeup and then hobbled back to the table. When she got there, Tom was roaring mad. "What the f-f-f-f-hell, Annie!" he screamed at her as she approached the table. Everyone was looking at her and Tom. The whole room seemed suddenly to grow just a little bit quieter, and the energy all around them was focused right on their fight. Suddenly, it seemed to Annie as if Tom were playing to an audience. He strutted over to her, clearly furious.

"Where were you," he roared. "We've been trying to leave for half an hour! And you are nowhere to be found. What is up with that!!"

Annie managed to sit down at the table, and she threw her crutches down behind her chair. She could feel her cheeks flaming.

All of a sudden, she just couldn't take anymore. The leg, the cast, the embarrassment, the whole night just got on top of her. She looked at Tom, eyes blazing. "So go! You sure as hell don't care about my feelings. You got me something to eat and then you ran out of here as fast as you could. You've been dancing with these other girls the whole night. And they look at me like I'm not even worthy to sit at the table with them. And you—you seem to think the same thing! Why did you ask me to this stupid dance anyhow?" Even as Annie was speaking, she was a little bit shocked at herself. She never lost her temper in public, but this was just too much. She could feel herself blushing beet red, but for some reason, she just didn't care.

Tom came over and grabbed her arm, a little roughly, and sat down beside her. He looked like he was about to explode. "You are just way too young," he said. "I don't know what I was thinking. You might look like you're all grown up, but you aren't. And I am too old for you. I never should have asked you to this dance. I am way too mature for you." Annie thought he sounded really stupid.

"And way too cool. And way too experienced. And way too wonderful," Annie sneered at him. She could feel tears gathering at the edges of her eyes. She willed them not to fall.

"Well, since you mention it. I wasn't going to go there, but you're absolutely right," Tom sneered right back at her. Once again, Annie had the distinct impression that he was performing for an audience.

Everyone around them was sort of pretending that they weren't watching, but casting sideways glances at the two of them just the same.

Annie lost her battle with the tears, and they started to fall down her cheeks. "Take me home," she said, grabbing her crutches from behind her chair.

"Gladly," said Tom. He turned to the other people at the table, all of whom were still watching the fight as though it were some amusing little soap opera. The girls' faces were carefully blank and emotionless, but Annie felt like she could hear their thoughts racing. One girl, she forgot which one she was, asked Tom if they would see him later. He said, "As soon as I deliver Princess Annie safely back to her father I'll catch up with all of you at the after party. Save me a cold one."

So, Annie thought, he was planning on going to an after party, which he had never even mentioned to her. And it sounded like he planned on drinking. Fine. She was way past ready to go home anyhow. They walked out to the parking lot as soon as the gates opened for dismissal, if you could call it that. Kids were streaming out to cars and party limousines, hired for the night.

Once again, Tom told her to wait on the sidewalk as he went to get the car, but it didn't have the same feeling as it had earlier in the evening. Annie felt discarded and disheveled. Worn out and dirty. Her ankle was throbbing and her blue dress had several snags in it. Tom pulled the car around and she got in. They did not speak the whole way home. When he got to her house, it was just past 10:30. Her father would be surprised to see her home so early. In disgrace.

Tom pulled up her driveway and came around and opened her car door. She had dried her tears and composed her face. He walked beside her while they walked up the sidewalk. As soon as her father opened the door, he turned around and said goodnight. Annie didn't say anything. Her dad raised his eyebrows in surprise. He helped Annie hobble in and said, "Don't get me wrong. I'm delighted to see you, but I'm also just a little bit surprised. I didn't think I would see you until about a minute before your curfew. If then." He spoke very quietly, and there was a question in his tone of voice.

Annie hobbled over to the couch, and he sat down beside her. She sort of collapsed in his arms, crying softly. He held her gently, saying nothing. Annie looked at him and said, "Things did not go very well. I think he wished he had never invited me. I couldn't dance, and I am just a freshman. Which he mentioned several times during the night. And I am not cool like the people he usually hangs with. He could hardly wait to get rid of me. And we had a fight, and everyone watched." Things started pouring out of Annie. Every time she thought she was done speaking, another sentence came, all mixed with hiccups and tears.

Her dad held her still, but he lifted her face so he could look right in her eyes. He said, "Annie. Listen to me, and listen hard. Are you ready?" She nodded. "This too shall pass," he said wisely.

"What does that mean?" Annie sniffed.

"You think about it, and you will figure it out. And then I want you to remember it because one day you will have to say the very same words to your daughter or son. I would bet a hundred dollars on it.

190

This too shall pass. Now, hobble yourself upstairs and get into your PJ's. I will bring you up a cup of hot chocolate. And let me tell you something else. You are very, very cool. Too cool for Tom Marino and his Barbie Dolls. Way too cool." He kissed her on the forehead and sent her up to her room. She took a long, hot shower, hanging her leg outside the shower stall. She just stood there in the hot water and washed the whole night off. When she came into her room, her dad had set a little tray on her bed, with a shortbread cookie and a cup of hot chocolate. And it was still hot.

Chapter 23

Annie was absolutely sure that everyone would be talking about her on Monday morning when she got to school. How she and Tom got into a shouting match. She had been preparing herself for a battle all morning. So, she was very surprised when absolutely nobody was talking about it at all. It was kind of like it had never happened. She had a hard time figuring that out until she realized, all of a sudden, that everybody had their own problems, and her own particular problems didn't figure all that prominently in their Monday morning thoughts.

Annie was surprised to see Zoe back at school, and she hobbled over to welcome her back. Zoe looked like she thought that everybody would be talking about her too, but they weren't. It was just the regular Monday morning buzz, and from what Annie could tell, most of the boys were talking about football. The Detroit Lions had a decent team this year, and it was just about all they seemed to care about this morning.

Annie said to Zoe, "Welcome back. I think we might finish *The Old Man and the Sea* today. So, if you want to borrow my book or talk about the book, just let me know. I'll be happy to help." Zoe nodded her thanks and looked at Annie's cast. "When do you get that off?" she asked.

Annie said, "I have a doctor appointment in a couple of days, and he is going to do another x-ray. If things look good, I might just have to have it wrapped. Fingers crossed. I am really sick of this stupid, heavy cast. And even more sick of these crutches."

Zoe said, "I heard you went to Homecoming with Tom Marino. He's kind of a big deal, isn't he? How did that go?"

Annie smiled sadly and said, "Absolutely terrible. The worst night you could imagine. He thought he was way too cool for me and could hardly wait to get rid of me. He ditched me and danced with just about every other girl there." She was surprised at how easily the truth came out. She was afraid that Zoe would laugh at her, but instead she had the feeling that Zoe was laughing with her.

Zoe laughed softly and said, "What a loser. I had a sneaking suspicion he might be a jerk."

Annie grinned and crutched her way over to her desk and sat down. Mrs. Murphy called the class to order, worked through a couple of announcements, and then said, "Let's finish up with the old man today." Annie thought that she saw Mrs. Murphy smile at Zoe, but she didn't say anything.

"Let's pick up with day three of the novel. Poor old Santiago has been awake for three days now, battling this enormous fish. His hands are cramped and bloody. Some critics say that Santiago has become something of a Christ-figure, with the bloody wounds on his hands echoing the crucifixion wounds of Christ. I am not going to pursue that imagery any further than to mention it to you so that you know about the possibility. You can use it if you think it is relevant, and you do not have to use it at all if you do not. Also, Santiago has been isolated for a very long time. The people of the village stay away from him, since he is supposed to be a man of bad luck, and they do not want his bad luck to rub off on them. The other day we were talking about the moment where the marlin jumps clear out of the water, showing Santiago his magnificent size, and Santiago said to himself that he admires the fish very much, but will kill him just the same. Do you all remember?" The class nodded their assent, and Mrs. Murphy asked, "Then what?"

Annie felt like keeping a low profile for some reason, so she sat quietly and watched and listened. A boy at the back of the room, a boy named Mike Something, raised his hand and said, "Then sharks."

A simple, declarative statement. But effective. Annie turned around to glance at him. Mrs. Murphy said, "You're right. Then sharks. And they are a game changer, aren't they? Would you like to go on and tell us what happens?"

Mike said, "Well, the old man does battle with the sharks. He kills the first one, but then they come in packs. They come at sunset and then in the darkness. He fights them, clubbing where he thinks the sharks might be. Eventually, they rip the club out of his hands, and he is defenseless. He hears the sharks devour all the meat off of his beautiful marlin, and there is nothing he can do to stop them. He is left with just the skeleton of the great fish that he has killed. He doesn't feel like he won anything. In fact, he feels nothing at all. Just numb."

Annie thought about what he had said. She decided that he had said it perfectly. The poor old man felt numb. Just numb. Annie looked at Mike with newfound respect and appreciation. Annie thought to herself that in this school, it was still cool to be smart. And that was very cool, too.

Mrs. Murphy said, "Very nicely done, Mike. Can anyone take it from there?" Everyone was quiet for a minute. Then, Olivia raised her hand. Mrs. Murphy smiled at her. "Yes, Olivia? Take us home."

Olivia said, "He feels the current grab his little boat, and he recognizes the shoreline. He knows he can get home now, but he admits to himself that he had made a big mistake. He went out too far. He knows that he has lost the battle, and all he really wants is his bed. He arrives in the harbor and pulls up his boat, leaving the remains of the big fish tied to the boat, too tired to care."

"Very good," said Mrs. Murphy. "The passage you are referring to is such an important one, Olivia. Well done. And in the morning, the villagers discover his boat, and they see the great skeleton of the marlin, which they measure. All of the men of the village are impressed. It was eighteen feet long. But, tell me about Manolin. What does he do?"

Brandon put up his hand. "All he really cares about is Santiago. Manolin runs to him, and Santiago says that he was beaten by the sharks. Manolin reminds him that he was not beaten by the great fish. He was defeated by a gang of bullies, not in one to one competition. He brings Manolin coffee and newspapers and food. It's clear that Manolin doesn't care what anybody says. He has decided that he is going to fish with Santiago from now on. As long as he can. And while he is running around taking care of him, Santiago is safe in his bed, dreaming of lions." Brandon smiled. "I really liked that ending. To me, it was like he was dreaming of his youth, when he was young and strong. So, I guess I would say that in some way, he has been healed or something—in a way."

Mrs. Murphy smiled. "It sounds to me like you are already thinking about the great essay you want to write on this book." She said this with a happy twinkle in her eye, and then she handed out essay prompts. "Here you are. Let's take a look at these questions. The essay is due one week from today. 600 words is your minimum. You must use at least five quotes from the text of the novel to support what you say." Then, she worked through the questions with the class. Annie tried to concentrate on what everyone was saying, but her thoughts kept circling back to one question. Had he been defeated or not? She glanced down the list of questions to see if that was there. The class was discussing the topics, but Annie was lost in her own little world. Her eyes ran down the page: What is the role of the sea? Discuss the religious symbolism. Discuss the symbolism of the lions. And then, there it was. The very question she had been hoping for.

"A man can be destroyed but not defeated," says Santiago after the first shark attack. At the end of the story, is the old man defeated or not? Defend your answer. That is the one. The question that had been haunting Annie. She felt a little frisson of happiness that she had already predicted the question. As if it proved to her that she got it. But she also realized that it was very important to explain what Hemingway meant by "destroyed" and "defeated." The bell rang, and Annie realized that she had not been paying attention. The class was suddenly over, and she wasn't entirely sure when the essay was due. Next Monday, she heard. Her ankle throbbed quietly as she struggled to her feet and grabbed her crutches.

Santiago was in her head for the rest of the morning. She hobbled through the halls, certain that she was seeing sneers on the faces of the upperclassmen that she passed. The hopeful feeling she had had for a moment, when she had correctly predicted the essay question, seemed to disappear as the day went on.

A feeling of drudgery had set in instead. The weekend seemed to be a million miles away. Two more weeks of the cast and the crutches. Hopefully. She wished that she too, just like Santiago, could be sound asleep in her bed, dreaming of lions. She almost smiled to herself, realizing that she probably wouldn't be dreaming about lions, and she wondered what her equivalent of "lions" might be.

Chapter 24

That weekend there was a party, and somehow Annie got invited. Word of mouth. And so did Olivia. It was at the same house that had hosted the wild party that Annie had been to earlier in the fall, the one she had told Olivia all about. So, needless to say—Olivia was determined to go to this one, no matter what. Annie had a weird feeling that it would be better to pass it up. She had to write her essay for English, and she was still on her stupid crutches. And there is no way a girl can feel sexy on crutches. But Olivia was not to be dissuaded. She talked Annie into staying the night at her house on Saturday night, and the two of them would go to the party, and they would be driven there by Annie's driver, and they would be picked up and brought home and everything would be fine. Annie's father said she could go, but he stipulated that she should not be out later than midnight, and she agreed.

So, Saturday evening, Annie pulled up in her big Mercedes, and her dad met Pierre, and Annie hobbled out and got in the car. When they got to Olivia's house, Olivia spent a lot of time on Annie's hair and makeup. Annie never spent any time at all on that, and she had to admit that what Olivia did with her eyes was really pretty. Olivia understood how to do contouring and highlighting, and things like that, and when Annie looked in the mirror, she saw someone who looked older than her. Olivia's mom was out on a date, or book club, or something, so when they were ready, they had no one to judge their outfits but the driver, Pierre. When he saw them come downstairs, he raised his eyebrows at Olivia. But she ignored his questioning look and gave him the address of the party. "Good evening, young ladies. I have strict instructions to pick you up at 11:30 at the front of the house where this party is. Do we understand that?"

"Yes, sir," Annie said. "We understand. That works for me because my dad said I had to be home at Olivia's by midnight." Pierre assisted her with her crutches, getting her settled comfortably in the back seat of the beautiful car. Olivia connected her phone to the Bluetooth in the car and started playing music. Annie could see Pierre silently cringe at the music selection, but he said nothing, of course.

They arrived at the party, and he reminded them of the pickup time. Annie felt a little bit like Cinderella going to the ball. Pierre was a funny stand-in for a fairy godmother, but he seemed to be playing that role tonight. As she and Olivia went around to the back of the house, the party was in full swing. It was a different scene than back in the fall. The pool had a cover over it,

the summer long since past. But, there were
tables of snacks and a keg in the dark corner
of the yard. There were couples dancing
and flirting. Annie looked around and saw
some of the upperclassmen she had met
through running and through her brief time
with Tom. None of them paid any attention
to her, or so it seemed.

To be honest, Annie couldn't be
certain if they were snubbing her or if they
were just too busy with their own stories.
She realized that some other freshmen had
been invited, too, because she saw Dylan
surrounded by some very pretty girls. No
surprise. He seemed older than he was.
And she saw several other kids from her
classes—Tiffany, Alexis, Mike, Paul. There
were probably more. A cute guy from their
English class named Nick came over to talk
to them, but it was clear to Annie that he had
his eye on Olivia.

"Hey," he said. "You want a beer?"
Olivia blushed and giggled. "Um,"
she said. "I've never had a beer. Are you
sure it's ok?" Annie said nothing, but then,
Nick wasn't really talking to her, and she
was painfully aware of that fact.

"Sure. You can just have one. It's
early in the evening. It will all wear off
before you go home. I'll be right back.
Here, hold this cup for me." He handed
Olivia a red Solo cup full of beer.

She took a sip and licked her lips. She grinned at Annie. "Here, take a sip. It's actually not horrible." Annie felt so out of place and so lonely that she took a sip. Even as she did it, she realized that her reason for doing so made no sense at all, but she really just didn't care at that particular moment.

Suddenly, Nick was back with two Solo cups, one for her and one for Olivia. He took his own cup back from Olivia and raised his cup in a mock salute. "Cheers," he said. "I suspect that you two are losing your beer virginity at this very moment. What a lucky guy am I to have two virgins at once." Olivia blushed and giggled again, but Annie scowled. It seemed like such a stupid and egotistical thing to say. He must have noticed Annie's look because he quickly said to Olivia, "Hey, come over here. I want to introduce you to someone. We'll be right back."

Olivia looked at Annie and said, "Will you be all right by yourself for a minute? I'll be back soon."

Annie pulled herself together. "I'm hardly by myself, Olivia. There must be over a hundred people here. I'll find someone to talk to until you get back. Go on." Olivia leaned in and gave Annie a quick kiss on the cheek and then turned and ran away with Nick. Annie stood there, feeling very much alone in spite of the many people swirling all around her, leaning on her crutches, and getting just a little bit chilly. It was November already, after all, and the autumn was losing its battle with winter.

In spite of the chill, the party was roaring. She could see several couples kissing and groping each other, and there was that guy over there, slipping his hand up under a girl's sweater. The girl was grinning at him. It was pretty clear that she knew that others were watching, and she was all too eager to give them a little bit of a show. He lifted her sweater and kissed her flat stomach. She giggled and pushed him away, but Annie was pretty sure she didn't mind. Other people were watching, too. Annie thought to herself that maybe they should get a room. She laughed bitterly and drank her beer. She looked around and saw couples laughing and kissing all around the patio, under the twinkling patio lights.

A cold wind blew, and she shivered. She wished she were home writing her essay. She felt stupid, awkward, and heavy. She drank her beer, just to have something to do as the music blasted over the party. She hobbled over to a chair and sat down, lifting the Solo cup and draining the last of her beer, trying not to look so conspicuously alone. She hadn't even realized that she had been drinking it. She stretched out her leg and tried to rub out a cramp in her thigh. She felt completely miserable, wondering how and where she fit in, if she fit in at all.

Suddenly, blue lights appeared in the sky, and sirens sounded. "Cops!" somebody shouted. "Cops!" Annie struggled to her feet, shouting for Olivia, who was nowhere to be seen. She dropped her cup and started to hobble toward the gate, having no clear idea of where to go or what to do. Everybody was running as fast as they could, hopping over fences at the back of the yard and disappearing into the night.

Oddly enough, as Annie looked around, there was one person running toward her. Dylan. There was no way Annie could run, so she just stood there in the backyard, feeling all alone, leaning on her stupid crutches.

Dylan took her hand in his and stood beside her as the policemen approached. Annie looked at him with panic in her eyes. He whispered, "Hang on. Hang on." Annie wondered what he was talking about.

All of a sudden, she saw Olivia running over to her, too. Annie was shocked. "What are you doing, Olivia? Why did you come back?"

Olivia looked terrified, but she said, "I'm not going to leave you all alone. And I knew you couldn't run with that thing on your leg." She had tears in her eyes, but she grabbed Annie's hand and hung on tightly.

Dylan smiled at Olivia. "Well, she wasn't alone. I was with her, but I think it's pretty cool that you came back for her." The three of them stood there in the middle of the big backyard, waiting for the inevitable—whatever that was.

They were suddenly confronted by two police officers who said, "Good evening, young people. You are coming with us to the police station. All of you. Have you got some ID?" Annie was stupefied. There were only about ten of them that had been caught. The rest had scampered into the night. Olivia was digging around in her little purse, looking for her ID, bravely fighting back tears. An officer guided Olivia away, into a squad car with some other kid. Annie was also ushered into a squad car, and they handed her crutches into her. Almost gently. Dylan was ushered into the same car. He sat beside her in the darkness, saying nothing. She started crying and couldn't stop. Dylan patted her once, gently on her arm. Then he held her hand lightly, but said nothing. Annie realized that there really wasn't anything to say. She also realized that this was the second time she had cried in front of Dylan.

When they got to the station, there were police officers all around under glaring fluorescent lights. Annie looked around for Olivia, but couldn't see her anywhere. The police station was a lot bigger than she had ever realized. Not that she had ever thought about it before. They asked her for some identification—which she didn't have—and then they called her dad.

Annie felt her heart drop right to the bottom of her feet. She was suddenly so heavy that she couldn't even stand up. She started thinking about her mom, and how disappointed she would be. Then, she realized that her dad would be here any moment, and she had no idea what she could say to him that could possibly explain what she had done.

He had told her a million times that she could not drink at these parties, that he was a teacher at the high school, and that everything she did reflected back on him. She had not even wanted the beer. It really hadn't even tasted good. The tears streamed silently down her face. Dylan put his arm around her shoulders as they sat side by side in hard plastic chairs. "This is not the end of the world, Annie," he said softly. She was surprised to hear a kind of tenderness in his voice. It was not a quality that she would have ever attributed to him. It reminded her a little bit of the time her dad had said 'this too shall pass.' But she did not think that was possible right now. The whole world seemed focused on this moment. The moment she had betrayed her dad's trust.

Ten minutes later, her dad walked in. Annie wondered who was watching the little kids. His hair was all messed up, and he looked like he had just thrown his jeans and a sweatshirt on. He did not look at all like her pulled-together Dad. He looked like a very sleepy, worried, and angry version of himself. Annie tried to find some words. She stammered, through tears, "Dad. I'm so sorry. I know you told me never to drink. Someone handed me a beer, and I was standing there, and I just drank it. It's the first time I've ever done that. Honestly." She felt incredibly stupid. Why should he believe anything she said?

"Just be quiet right now, Annie, and let's see what's going on," her father answered. He seemed very angry, working hard to control his anger with her. Furthermore, he seemed scared. That made it even worse.

Annie said, "Who's watching Sarah and Eddie?"

Her father looked at her, meaning for her to be quiet. "Mrs. Murphy came over." Oh no. Annie's shame grew even deeper. She liked Mrs. Murphy, and what would she think of her now? And then another thought entered her mind—wasn't it interesting that her dad called Mrs. Murphy when he needed someone to watch the kids, late at night. There must be something more going on between the two of them than just good friends, or colleagues. Annie realized that she had not been paying attention to much of anything but her own story. And she felt like such a loser. A policeman came over and escorted her and her father into a small room. He had Annie breathe into some strange contraption that Annie knew was a breathalyzer. She waited while the officer and her father talked together, both of them seeming to ignore her.

The police officer clearly knew her father, and he was respectful. He said, "Well, this shows that she is telling the truth, at least. She only had one beer. If that. Nonetheless, she is a minor, and there will be consequences for this. It can't be avoided." He spoke softly, but firmly.

Her father nodded and said, "I understand. Are we free to go home now? I have two other children at home." The officer said that they could go and that someone from the court would contact them about what happens next. Annie's father thanked him and escorted her out of the police station and into the family car. Annie realized, in passing, that she did not know what had happened to Dylan, or who had come to pick him up. Or Olivia. She started shivering and could not stop. She was cold, but these shivers were worse than that. Her dad was silent, maybe gathering his thoughts or deciding what to say. For Annie, his silence hung like daggers in the air.

She whispered, "Dad. I'm so sorry. I know I've let you down, and I don't even know why I did it. I am so, so sorry. I don't even know what to say. Please tell me you forgive me." She looked over at him, but he kept his eyes on the road, staring straight ahead. Annie felt her tears running freely down her face.

Her dad drove on in silence for a few minutes. He again seemed to be weighing his words. Then, he spoke, very quietly. "Annie, I'm disappointed. I know it's hard for you without your mom, and I know that you are trying to figure out a lot of things by yourself. But when you make bad decisions like you did tonight, they can have long lasting consequences, far beyond what you might think. I don't know what the ramifications of this will be. We will talk in the morning after I've had time to think. I want you to remember what I told you the other day—this too shall pass. It might not feel like it right now, but we will get through this. It's not the end of the world, even though it might feel like it right now. Now, take a hot shower and go to bed." Annie realized that her dad had just said the very same thing that Dylan had said to her. Interesting.

They walked in the house, and Mrs. Murphy was in the front room, reading a book. She didn't say a word. Just nodded to Annie. With a sad little smile on her face. Annie went up to her room, grateful that the little kids were already in bed. She shut her door and heard voices from the living room—her dad and Mrs. Murphy talking. She could not hear what they were saying, but then, she didn't want to either. She stripped off her clothes, hung her bad leg outside the shower curtain, and turned the water on as hot as she could stand it. She got in bed and said her prayers, which basically consisted of talking to her mom, telling her how sorry she was. Then, she surprised herself by falling asleep. Small mercies.

Chapter 25

In the morning, when she got up, Eddie and Sarah did not seem any different. Maybe they just did not know anything about last night. Annie would be grateful if it could stay that way. When she came into the kitchen, her dad was on the phone, talking with someone about her. She poured herself a cup of coffee, adding lots of cream and sugar. She brought the coffee pot over to where her father was sitting at the kitchen table, and she poured a little into his cup to warm his coffee up. He was wrapping up his call. She sat and waited for the news. She remembered how much her mom had loved her morning cup of coffee. Her mom used to say that for her, the morning always started better with a cup of coffee. Annie had started to drink it during the past year. For Annie, the coffee had to be cut with lots of cream and sugar, but it still seemed like a connection to her mom. Like a way of saying good morning to her. And this morning, Annie felt like she needed her by her side, more than ever. Her dad said goodbye to whoever he was talking to, hung up, and looked at Annie.

"I guess I don't have to tell you again how disappointed I am by what happened last night. Bad decisions." He cleared his throat, searching for his next words.

Before he could speak again Annie said, "Dad. Honestly. I am so sorry. I know you're disappointed in me, and that's the worst punishment. But the truth is, I am also disappointed in myself. I really don't know why I did it. I didn't intend to drink anything, and then I just did."

He put his hand up to stop her. "I know. I know. But like we said last night, there will be consequences. I just got off the phone with the police department. You have to go there after school this Monday and stand in front of a judge who is going to talk to you about consequences. I figure the sooner the better, because if you're anything like me, and I think you are, you will have no peace of mind until you know what this whole episode is going to cost you. And it is going to cost you something." Annie said nothing, but she couldn't help but think about all of the kids that had escaped "consequences," including all of those who had run out of the yard, jumping fences, and disappearing into the night.

She thought about saying something to that effect, but wisely decided that there was no point in going there. Her father said, "I have a good friend who is an attorney, Mr. Hadley. You remember him? He is going to come with us to this meeting. He is very well connected in the court system, and it might help." Annie looked at her dad, and she could feel tears gathering at the corners of her eyes again. She thought about Olivia, both of whose parents were attorneys. They could handle Olivia's case for free. She wondered if she should ask Olivia if they could help her.

"Is this going to cost you a lot of money? Do you think I should ask Olivia if her parents could help us out?" she asked softly. She knew that there wasn't a lot of extra money in the budget.

Her father said, "No. That's all right. This man is a good friend, and about the money—let me worry about that. As for you, I think you have a big essay to write today. As I recall, it's due Monday. You worry about that. Do a good job. Mrs. Murphy tells me that you have been doing a great job in her class, and I don't want you to get sidetracked and screw up your grade in there. One of the things that Mr. Hadley will be telling the judge is that you are a good student. Let's make sure it's true." He reached over and kissed her on the cheek and added, "Yes. I am very disappointed with what you did last night. But I love you. I love you, and most of the time, I am very proud of you. What you did was stupid, but it is not a sin that puts you beyond redemption. If I remember *The Scarlet Letter* correctly, that is an important theme, right?"

Annie brought her eyes up to meet his. She was astonished that he knew anything about *The Scarlet Letter*. Startled, she said, "I didn't think you knew that story, Dad."

He smiled a little smile at her and said, "Oh, who could ever forget the lusty Hester Prynne. The image of her standing outside that prison door with a beautiful baby in her arms is not something a man forgets very easily. Now, get some breakfast and get to work on your essay. It is Sunday, and I think we shall go to church and pray for your eternal soul. And then I have some football to watch, and you, as I said, have an essay to write. One thing at a time, Miss Annie." She looked at him in astonishment, not quite able to decide if his tone was light-hearted or serious. She decided that it was a little bit of both. She finished her coffee, got a breakfast bar, gave him a quick hug and went upstairs to get ready for church.

Chapter 26

At church, there had been a reading about entering by the narrow gate. Annie hadn't really paid very close attention to the reading, but the image of the narrow gate stayed in her head for some reason. First, she thought about the narrow gate to the railroad tracks, the trail where she had tripped and hurt herself. She remembered that there was that one day last fall when she had thought she had heard a strange buzzing there. Must have been the bees. She remembered that, at the time, she thought that the buzzing was all tied up with her remembering her mother's voice, and the way she sang the old Scottish song. My luve is like a red, red rose.

Then, her mind started playing with the image of the narrow gate. Maybe it was a symbol, or a metaphor. Maybe, the narrow gate could stand for something. Maybe, Santiago had entered the narrow gate when he sailed out too far. He had made a mistake, and he had been punished for it. But, he was not destroyed. Or, would Hemingway say defeated? She had to figure that part out. But one thing was clear. At the end of the book, he is once again respected by the people of the village. He is lying in his bed dreaming of lions. Her mind went back to the image of the narrow gate.

Maybe, you have to lose before you can win, or you have to be hurt—really hurt—before you can know some kind of peace. She remembered what Mrs. Murphy had said about the sacred hurt. The kind of hurt that makes you reevaluate everything. A hurt where you've lost your innocence, and you know it. The world is different on the other side of that kind of hurt. Maybe the narrow gate is suffering, and the beginning of understanding is on the other side of it. The idea kind of worked, because when you are hurting, it almost feels like your heart is being squeezed. The narrow gate.

All of these ideas kept running around in her head, and she wrote the longest essay she had ever written. The words simply flew out of her fingers, just like her dad said her mom used to write. She wondered if she was imagining it, or if she really was feeling some spiritual connection to her mom. She worked for hours, but the time flew by, and she felt pretty good about what she had written.

A man can be destroyed but not defeated. She figured out what Hemingway meant. A man can be destroyed, that is killed. All men will die, and in that way, be destroyed. But, if he keeps to his code of honor and comes through any battle with his dignity intact, then he is not defeated. She had discovered that she knew a little bit more about what it feels like to sail out too far, just like poor Santiago had done. She had sailed out too far last night. She only hoped that she would not be destroyed or defeated by what she had done.

She only took time out for a quick phone call from Olivia, who told her how sorry she was. Her parents were mad, but they were going to handle her case. Just like Annie thought. They both felt pretty stupid about the whole scene last night. A little disappointed in themselves. And embarrassed. Then, they talked a little while about the idea of the sacred hurt, and Olivia said that she had not connected the two ideas until Annie explained it to her. She told Annie that their conversation was going to help her write a better essay. Annie said she felt the same way.

When she got to school in the morning and turned in her essay, Mrs. Murphy kindly made no reference to the weekend. She just smiled a very tiny smile at Annie and accepted her essay. And Olivia's too. Dylan turned in his essay too. He smiled at Annie, but he said nothing about the night before. Then Mrs. Murphy got the class going on some selections of poetry for the hour. She told them that they were going to study a few of the most famous Shakespearean sonnets. Although Annie was interested, she had a hard time concentrating. Her mind kept going to the appointment she had after school that day, with her dad and Mr. Hadley. And the judge.

Eventually, the day was finally over, and it was time to face the music. Before they went in, Mr. Hadley came over and sat with them. He introduced himself to Annie, and she remembered that she had met him once before, at her mother's funeral. He said, "Hi, Annie. I'm sorry that we are getting together under these particular circumstances, and I know that you are a very good student and a very good daughter, and that you are not likely to do anything like this again. Am I right?" He had dark, curly hair, and a twinkle in his eyes.

"No, sir," Annie said. "I will never do anything like this again."

Mr. Hadley laughed and said, "Well, let's not go too far. But remember, you are only fifteen, and you have a lot of growing up to do still. And you are way too young to be drinking. So, let's take it cool. Now, I had your dad as my physics teacher a long time ago, and he is a man I really admire. So, he and I have been talking. And we have a plan. I'm going to go in there before you and your dad, and I'm going to have a little talk with Judge Miller, who is also a former student of your dad's. A little talk, off the record. And when I'm done, I will call you and your dad in. I want you to assure Judge Miller that you understand that what you did was wrong, and that it will not happen again. You got that?"

Annie said, "Yes, sir." She and her dad sat on hard plastic chairs, and Mr. Hadley went in to see the judge. Annie said, "Is he charging you a lot of money, Dad? I'm so sorry about this. It bugs me that so many other kids got off clean, and I got caught."

Her father looked at her very sternly and said, "Let's not lose focus here, Annie. What you did was wrong. I don't care about those other kids. I care about you. You broke faith with me. And Mr. Hadley is doing this for free, because I was his teacher, and a long time ago, I helped pull him through physics, which was not his forte." Annie looked at her dad gratefully, realizing how much he must matter to his former students if they would do something like this for free. Annie realized that she often took her dad for granted.

Suddenly, Mr. Hadley came out of the room and came over to them. He said, "All right. Let's go see the judge." Annie grabbed her crutches and started to hobble over to the room, with her dad and Mr. Hadley following. They entered the judge's chambers, and he motioned for her to sit down, right across from his desk. She did so, setting her crutches on the floor beside her chair.

He looked at her, rather sternly. "How did you hurt yourself, Annie?" Annie gulped, having been caught off guard by the question. "I fell running on the track sir. I mean, not the track. The old railroad tracks that we use for a cross-country trail. I missed the last races of the season because of that stupid fall."

The judge said, "Well, Annie. Let's just take a moment and think about what you have just said. You said that the fall was stupid, and that because of it, you had to miss the last races of the season. From what you've said, it's clear to me that you understand that actions have consequences. Or, as your father taught me, actions cause reactions. This is true in the world of physics, in the world of running, and in the real world as well." He looked hard at Annie to make sure that she was paying attention. She was. She realized, almost in passing, that the judge was speaking in metaphors, too. She was listening very carefully. She sat silently, looking right at him, her dad sitting beside her. She could feel her heart beating in her chest.

He continued, "Now, I have spoken to your English teacher, Mrs. Murphy, and she tells me that you are one of her best students. Your other teachers have all agreed with this assessment. I personally know your father, having been his student long ago, and Mr. Hadley tells me that you are a very good young lady who has just made one mistake. I am aware that you lost your mom a couple years ago, and I'm sure that has been hard for you."

Annie sat there, listening carefully as this description was presented to her. She felt tears gathering at the corners of her eyes again, but she said nothing, and she did not raise her hand to wipe away the tears that were forming. Judge Miller went on, "Mrs. Murphy is the faculty advisor for a community service project at your school called Study Buddies. She has open, free tutoring in her classroom after school two days a week. Students who are less gifted than yourself can come there and receive tutoring from a peer in any subject, but I understand that you are very good in English, so you will offer your services in that subject. You will report to Mrs. Murphy's room every Tuesday and Thursday after school for the next fifteen weeks. That will accumulate in thirty hours of community service, and I think that will be a fair recompense for your bad decision last weekend. Are you in agreement with this plan?"

Annie nodded and said, "Yes, sir. Thank you, sir." She felt a rush of gratitude, and she realized that she was getting off lightly.

Her father said, "Judge Miller, do I understand you correctly that, if Annie does this and fulfills this thirty hour commitment, there will be no record of this incident on her permanent record?" Annie was grateful that her father had asked this, because she didn't really feel like she could speak at the moment.

"Yes, Mr. Fitzsimmons. You do understand me correctly. It is late November now, so I will get a report from Mrs. Murphy in early April. By that time, you should have fulfilled your hours, Annie, and I personally will make sure that we never have to think about this incident again. Is that acceptable to you, Mr. Hadley? Mr. Fitzsimmons? Annie?"

"Yes, Judge Miller. We are in agreement with this plan. And thank you for your time," Mr. Hadley said. Her father added his agreement, and his gratitude.

Annie pulled herself together and said, "Thank you, sir. I won't let you down."

Judge Miller smiled and said, "I'm sure you won't." He then smiled at Annie's father. "Good to see you, sir. You've got a fine daughter there."

Mr. Hadley said goodbye to the judge, as did her father, and they left his chambers. Annie felt like a hundred pounds had been lifted from her shoulders. As soon as they were out of the judge's suite of rooms and they were in the clear, her dad put his arms around Annie, and she laid her head on his shoulder. Tears fell softly on his jacket. Then, Mr. Hadley and her dad shook hands, and her dad thanked Mr. Hadley again and again.

He said, "No problem. I'm glad that this whole episode had a happy ending, and I look forward to seeing both of you again someday, but under much happier circumstances."

Annie said, "Thank you, sir. For everything. I won't let you down." Mr. Hadley smiled and said that it was his pleasure. Annie's dad put his arm around her shoulder and took her out to the car. The wind was whipping, and Annie could feel winter waiting in the wings. The sky was gray, stripped of color, and the last leaves were being torn from the trees as they drove home. Thanksgiving was just around the corner, and once again, Annie was looking at the prospect of a big holiday without her mom. They stopped by the after-care room to pick up Eddie and Sarah.

Her dad surprised her by stopping by a pizzeria and ordering pizza. She looked at him in surprise, and he grinned, saying, "I think we both deserve a break after that. I don't feel like cooking dinner tonight, and I bet you don't, either. Let's celebrate your narrow escape from the clutches of the law. And, it is Monday night, so you know what that means. Monday night football."

Annie was so grateful and so exhausted that she sat and watched the first half of the game with her dad that evening, but she could not remember in the morning who had played or what the score was. When she woke up, it was Tuesday morning, and that meant it was the first day to report to after school tutoring with Mrs. Murphy.

Chapter 27

In English class, Mrs. Murphy said that this was just a three-day week because this Thursday was Thanksgiving, and the school had a four-day weekend. Annie knew that Thanksgiving was coming, but it had been able to sneak up on her since she was so preoccupied with her own drama lately. Maybe, too, she just hadn't allowed herself to think about it because the prospect of the holiday season without her mom still hurt so much. Mrs. Murphy said that she would be working on poetry today and tomorrow, but that after their Thanksgiving break, they were going to read *Twelfth Night,* a Shakespearean festive comedy. She warned them that the play was a little bawdy, and she said she hoped that they could all handle that.

She also said that the play had a very subtle Christmas subtext, an undercurrent that connected it to the Christmas season, so she thought it would be just the right thing for the last three weeks before Christmas break. As she explained all this, the class was buzzing—whether about the possibility of reading something a little bit "bawdy," or about Christmas coming, or even about Thanksgiving. Annie wasn't sure what was causing most of the reaction, but she sank a little lower in her seat. Suddenly, all she could think of was that it was about to be

Thanksgiving, and that holiday was all about her mom.

Her mom used to love to make the big turkey dinner, with all the trimmings. Every year, she tried out a new recipe for the dressing, and every year it was wonderful. And pies. And cranberry sauce. Her poor dad didn't know how to cook at all. Last Thanksgiving, they had gone to his mom's house, and her grandma had bravely prepared the feast. But all of them kept feeling the empty place at the table. The year before—right after her mom had died— Annie didn't even remember anything about that Thanksgiving. Or that Christmas, for that matter. The holidays had been a blur of pain and loneliness. She remembered that her dad had got them all presents, but that nothing seemed to matter.

Now, it had been two years and two months since her mom had died. Annie knew that she had to let healing come. She could feel her dad trying to do that, even in the hopeful little flirtation with Mrs. Murphy. She knew it had been about five years since her husband had passed away, so Mrs. Murphy probably needed to let healing come too. Annie remembered how she felt when she wrote her essay, when she felt her mom's spirit, confidence, and joy come into her fingers. She wondered if she was imagining that, or if it had really happened. She hadn't been paying attention to anything

Mrs. Murphy was saying, and she suddenly started listening again.

Mrs. Murphy was reminding all of them to go by the bookstore and pick up a copy of *Twelfth Night* by next Monday, reminding them that they would do a couple more poems tomorrow. As the bell rang and Annie gathered her things, Mrs. Murphy quietly said, "I'll see you today after school for Study Buddies, right?" There was nothing accusatory in her tone, but Annie blushed just the same. She said, "Yes. I will see you then. Have a good day, Mrs. Murphy."

After the school day was over, she went down to her dad's room to check in with him and remind him that she had her first tutoring session that day. She reminded him that she would come to his room in an hour, and asked if he would wait for her so she could have a ride home. He reminded her of something she had completely forgotten about. Today, she had a doctor appointment at five o'clock, and she might be able to get that stupid blue cast off. She could not believe that she had somehow forgotten this, but she hobbled down to Mrs. Murphy's class with a little bit of a lighter heart.

When she entered the classroom, there were seven small groups of students already working. She apologized for being a couple minutes late, telling Mrs. Murphy that she had had to go see her dad and remind him to wait for her. Mrs. Murphy said, "No problem at all. You're right on time. Annie, this is Ezekiel. He plays tight end for our football team, and you may have noticed him wreaking havoc on the football field this season. As you know, our team is in the playoffs this year, and Zeke needs to keep his grades up. But, also, as you know, since you are an athlete yourself, it's really hard when you have practice every night. Zeke needs some help with a grammar lesson, and I think you might be just the right person to help. Why don't you take those two desks in the back corner?"

Zeke grinned at her and offered to carry her books or her backpack. "I've been on those things myself," he said, gesturing to her crutches, "and I know they are no fun." They got settled in two desks at the rear of the classroom, and he opened up his notebook.

Annie surprised herself by actually feeling pretty comfortable talking to him. He was a senior, and a bigshot on the football team. Big man on campus, and all that stuff. Going to go to college on a football scholarship. But one on one, he just seemed like a nice guy. His skin was very dark, and her winter paleness had already set in, so their arms, coming together, looked like day and night. He had beautiful white teeth and a big smile that came easily to him. "I think I might get this thing off tonight," Annie said, "and I can't wait. I hate it, and don't ask me why I chose blue. I couldn't tell you. Anyhow, what are we working on?"

Zeke flipped pages in his composition notebook. "I have a grammar quiz tomorrow, and I would really appreciate it if you could make sense of this stuff for me. Participles, gerunds, and infinitives." He sighed heavily. "I just don't get it at all."

"Yikes," said Annie. "I was hoping you would give me something easier than that!"

He smiled at her and said, "Oh, don't worry if you can't do it. Maybe I can get someone else to help me."

Annie held up her hand, studying his notes and saying, "Hang on. I didn't say that. My mom was an English teacher. I kind of grew up with this stuff. All right, it's all coming back to me now. I can do this."

Ezekiel said, "You said your mom *was* an English teacher. Not anymore?"

He looked at Annie. Annie gulped and said, "No. She died two years ago. From cancer."

Zeke looked embarrassed, saying, "Oh, man. I am so sorry. You're so young to have lost your mom."

Annie grinned, sadly, and said, "I'm older than I look, and losing her made me grow up kind of fast. I have two little siblings at home."

Zeke said, "I've got my mom, but I lost my dad about five years ago. He OD'd on drugs." He had trouble meeting Annie's eyes.

"Wow," Annie said softly. "Sacred hurts everywhere." Zeke looked at her and smiled softly. "Hey, I remember that. I had Mrs. Murphy for freshman English, too. That was a great story—that one about the old man and the big fish. But," he smiled at her, "now talk to me about gerunds."

Annie said, "O.K. It all comes down to this. It matters how the word is being used. My mom used to teach me to diagram sentences to help me understand. I know it's old-fashioned, but it helped me, and it might help you. Let's try it."

Zeke laughed and said, "If it's one thing I'm used to, it's diagrams. Nobody ever tried that before with me for these things, but I see a lot of x's and o's on the coach's chalkboard. So, show me a diagram."

Annie got a clean sheet of paper in his notebook and started diagramming. The hour went by so fast that she could not believe it when it was four o'clock. Mrs. Murphy stood up and announced that the session was over. Ezekiel thanked Annie and said that he finally understood these things for the first time. He said that he

230

would see her again, and that he really appreciated her help, and then he said goodbye to Mrs. Murphy and took off for practice.

Mrs. Murphy asked Annie if she had enjoyed tutoring. Annie said, "I really did. It made me feel great that I could explain something to someone and they actually seemed to get it." She got her things together and said goodbye to Mrs. Murphy, excited about the possibility of getting her cast off.

Chapter 28

Annie was a little surprised with how shriveled her leg looked. It had been in the cast for almost five weeks, and the muscles had atrophied. However, the x-ray gave her a clean bill of health, and the doctor said that she could start running again. He cautioned her to take it slow in the beginning, and to listen to her body.

It was Thanksgiving morning, and the little kids were downstairs watching the Macy's Parade and the Detroit Parade in the living room while her dad bravely wrestled with a turkey. He grinned at her when she came downstairs in running gear.

"Are you going out for a run?" he asked, his hands covered in butter and seasoning as he glanced up from stuffing the turkey.

"I thought I would give it a try," Annie answered. "Don't worry, Dad. I remember what the doctor said, and I'll take it cool. I'm only going to try for two miles today, and I promise that I will take it slow. Then, I'll be back to help you with dinner preparations. Is anyone coming over today besides us?" She was secretly a little worried that he might have invited Mrs. Murphy, and although she really liked her, she just didn't feel like dealing with that complication today.

Her dad opened the oven and put the turkey in. Annie could see him heave a sigh of relief. "Well, your grandma is coming over. She's in charge of pies, so we don't have to worry about that. Anyhow, be careful. And by the way, I don't think you will need that heavy jacket. It is unseasonably warm out there today." He squinted his eyes to look through the window at the outside thermometer. "It's 55 degrees already, and it's going up to 60. Good day for a run. Bad for the stores who want everyone to start their Christmas shopping. By the way, I need a list from you."

He smiled at her. He was so brave, Annie thought. Her mom was the one who did all the Christmas shopping in the past. Annie suspected that her dad was still terrified of the awesome responsibility of buying presents for the three kids, but he was soldiering on with the task. Eddie and Sarah had already given him lists. Lists that he was passing on to Santa Claus, of course. Annie was pretty sure that Eddie didn't believe any more, but Sarah still did. The magic would only last a little bit longer for her, and her dad was trying very hard to make sure that she still had some time of innocence. Annie kissed him on the cheek and stepped out into the sunlight.

The trees were mostly stripped bare, and the sun shone through their branches with a surprising warmth. Annie left her jacket on the porch, also stripping off her scarf and mittens. Her dad was right. It was a lot warmer than she thought it would be. She walked down the sidewalk and tentatively tried a few steps on her new leg. It felt all right. She started to run with a nice, easy pace, almost afraid to believe that she could do it. Gradually, her stride lengthened, and she felt herself starting to run a little more smoothly. She was breathing carefully, and it felt like she was monitoring all her body parts as she tried it all out again after a long time away from the act of running. It was a little scary, but she slowly let go and let her legs carry her.

It was very quiet on the streets since it was Thanksgiving morning. Everyone was inside, having that second cup of coffee or watching the parades. Or stuffing the turkey and baking the pies. Annie's mind drifted back to her mom once again. She had so many memories of her mom making the Thanksgiving feast. She had often come downstairs to find her mom peeking in the oven, loving all the ceremonies of cooking, even the basting of the bird. Her mom loved Thanksgiving, because, even though it was a holiday in its own right, it was also the unofficial start of the Christmas season, and her mom loved everything about Christmas. The only sounds this morning were the swish of an occasional car passing by on the pavement, and the song of early morning birds. The air itself seemed to be holding its breath, allowing this surprisingly warm day when it was least expected.

Annie suddenly found herself at the entrance to the old train tracks. At the narrow gate. The earth seemed warm and dry here, and the grass seemed to make a cushion at the entrance to the tracks—the place where she had fallen. Annie knew that was the turn-around point for a two-mile run, so that meant that she had already run a mile. She felt pleased to recognize that she felt all right, that she wasn't hurting anywhere, that her leg felt stronger than she had thought it would. She sat down on the warm clump of grass, leaning her back against the narrow gate. She started thinking about what she had thought of the other day—that the narrow gate could be a symbol, or a metaphor. That she had entered by the narrow gate, and she had fallen. That because of that fall she had suffered. She closed her eyes and listened for the buzzing that she had heard so long ago, but all was quiet. The wild rose bush had one blossom still clinging to its vines, tucked under some dried grasses, and by some miracle, today it was blooming.

Then, her mind started playing with all of those images, and a new kind of understanding started forming at the edges of her consciousness. She was thinking about the narrow gate as a symbol for a passage into a kind of wisdom. The gate was still just a gate, an entrance to the railroad tracks, but it might be something more too, at the same time. She was thinking that losing her mom was—in a way—the narrow gate through which she had passed. That losing her was a sacred hurt, to use the words she had learned in her English class. That because of that sacred hurt, she had lost some things—some important things. She had lost her innocence, in a way, and her trust that everything would always be all right. She had lost her mom, and she missed her every day. She realized that she had recently made some mistakes, whether out of self-pity or carelessness, she wasn't entirely sure. But that she had also stood up for herself, and that she was healing. She had just run a mile, and she felt all right. She closed her eyes in the sunlight and let her mind drift. Before she knew it, she had fallen asleep, and she did not know how long she had been asleep. But she was suddenly awakened by a sound. Not a buzzing. More like the crack of a stick.

She opened her eyes carefully, but did not move. She looked into the woods, at the edge of the path leading up to the tracks. There, standing not more than ten feet away from her, was a doe and her baby fawn. They were standing very still, and both of them were looking at Annie. Annie was afraid to move. Or even breathe.

She gasped, almost startling them, and certainly startling herself. She wondered if they might charge at her, so she did not want to make them afraid enough to do anything like that. However, instead, they just stood there, seeming to stare at her in wonder. Slowly, Annie started breathing again. She very carefully lifted her hand, as if to wave hello. The mother seemed to dip her head, almost nod her head to Annie.

Then, she nudged her baby, and they turned around and disappeared back into the woods around the trail. Annie was astonished at how quickly they disappeared, their colors blending perfectly with the brown wood of the forest. She released her breath, almost afraid to move. Overcome with the beauty of it all. Trying to figure out if it meant anything, or if it was just a lucky accident. She pulled herself together and stood up, stretched out, and jogged home. She thought about telling her dad about what she had seen, and then she decided that she would keep it to herself. She needed to think about it before she could ever talk about it.

Chapter 29

Somehow, they got through the
Thanksgiving dinner, and it was really pretty
good. Her grandma had brought pumpkin
and apple pies, and she had pitched right in
with all the dinner preparations. After
dinner, her dad had settled gratefully into the
couch, slumbering and half-watching
football for the rest of the afternoon. The
rest of the four-day weekend slipped away
in a blur, with Eddie and Sarah studying the
sale flyers that came in the mail from toy
stores and video game stores. Sarah begged
Annie to help her write her letter to Santa,
detailing what she wanted. Even Eddie
asked her to help him get the list right,
telling Santa, or Dad—either way was fine
with him—what he wanted. They had each
written their Christmas lists before, but
given what they had seen in the sale flyers,
adjustments had to be made. Annie could
feel their excitement. All too soon, the four
days were up, and it was Monday, and
Annie was back in English class.

Mrs. Murphy explained that the
Shakespearean festive comedy was probably
going to be a little bewildering at first. She
said, "You see—a comedy is essentially a
journey. It begins in sadness and loss, moves
through a period of confusion, and arrives
finally at a new and better world, a place of
joy. You'll notice that I said the word 'joy'

instead of 'happiness,' and that was on purpose. It may be just my bias, but I have always felt that the word 'joy' expresses a deeper feeling than the word 'happiness.' Deeper, quieter, and more meaningful. I would like all of you to pull out a sheet of paper and take some notes while I give you some idea of the pattern of a comedy."

Everyone busily gathered pen and paper and looked up at Mrs. Murphy expectantly. She turned on the smart board at the front of the room, and the outline she was speaking about came up on the screen for all of them to see and copy. "You see," she said, "a comedy begins with a period of sadness. Lovers are dissatisfied or unhappy. Often, someone has lost a loved one and they are still grieving. Parents and children could be separated by bad luck or some evil tyrant. There could be a storm or some natural disaster. So, when the play begins, there isn't any joy."

A couple hands went up with questions about why a storm might matter. Mrs. Murphy said, "In this play, it's as if Shakespeare is suggesting that the natural world reflects the chaos or unhappiness of the human world. So—a storm. But then, the play moves into a period of confusion. Disguises often play a part in this confusion. One of Shakespeare's favorite devices is to have a young woman disguise herself as a young man, or a boy. And frequently, this disguise becomes so convincing that everyone thinks she really is this person she has invented. And then—to make matters worse—she meets the man of her dreams, but he thinks she's a boy, or a man!" Everyone giggled, and Gabriella raised her hand, excitedly.

"Oh, Mrs. Murphy! That sounds like the movie called *She's the Man!* I love that movie!" Gabriella said, almost bouncing in her seat.

"You're right!" Mrs. Murphy said. "That movie is a modern adaptation of this very play! And if you like, and if time permits, we might be able to watch it together before Christmas break." Dylan raised his hand from his desk at the back of the room.

"But, come on, Mrs. Murphy," he said, his voice dripping with sarcasm. "You don't really expect me to believe that a girl could disguise herself as a guy and be so convincing in this disguise that no one could see through it. No way a girl could be a guy that well. They don't understand us at all most of the time." Several of the other boys in the class chuckled and nodded, quietly agreeing with everything Dylan had said.

Mrs. Murphy smiled gently and said, "Well, Dylan. It's like you are anticipating my next point in my lecture. At this moment, I need to take a sidebar and tell all of you about a very important concept.

240

Something a famous poet called 'the willing suspension of disbelief.' The poet's name is Samuel Taylor Coleridge, and we will study his poetry later in the year, but suffice it to say that, in addition to being a poet, he was a Shakespearean scholar. And he said that in order to enter the spirit of a Shakespearean festive comedy, the reader—or audience— must engage in what he called the willing suspension of disbelief. In other words, you have an unspoken contract with the playwright, whereby you allow him or her some liberties, just for the pleasure of a good story. So, that part of your mind that says that a young woman could never successfully disguise herself as a young man—you agree to set that suspicion aside, just for the joy of the story." The way she said this, it almost seemed like she was implying that if you could not or would not do this, you were a fool. Everyone sat quietly and listened. Even Dylan.

"Now," she said. "Let's finish our outline. The third phase is the creation of a new and better world. In that final phase, disguises are dropped. That happens in almost every comedy. And, for this particular play, it brings about a very dangerous moment for our young heroine. Because the man she has fallen in love with thinks she's a boy. Maybe he thinks of her almost like a kid brother. And suddenly, she has to admit that she is not that at all. He might feel like she has betrayed his trust and want nothing more to do with her. Then, you have no joyful ending. Or, he might make another decision. And I will let you discover what that might be as we read this play together." The class rustled with excitement. "Furthermore," she added, "there are some moments of healing. Often, loved ones are reunited. Cruel people either have a change of heart or they are stripped of power. Sometimes, however, there is a character who has a chance to be happy, but he or she steadfastly refuses that opportunity."

She waited a minute to let this idea sink in. "Usually, that person storms off the stage, refusing to join the joyful dance at the end of the play. It's as if Shakespeare is acknowledging that there are some people who are just determined to be miserable. And there might be nothing anyone can do to change that. So," she shrugged her shoulders, "you just have to let them be. Now let me introduce the main characters to you and sort of give you a visual picture of each of them. Then, I'm going to assign parts. I've done a little planning for this, and I've chosen those of you who seem to like to read to read a part. If you would like to read and I haven't chosen you, please stay after class and see me. I'm not assigning all the parts today, because I've just chosen a few voices that I think might work for particular characters, and I will make the last selections tonight. So, let me know if you would like to read. Make sure you have your books tomorrow. And a highlighter." The class buzzed with excitement. They had never done a play together, reading parts out loud.

Mrs. Murphy described about six of the most important characters, so that they would know who they are and could picture them. Then, she said who would be reading each of the parts. Annie thought it would be fun to read Viola, who was clearly the main character in the play. But that part went to Gabriella, and Annie had to admit to herself that she would do it well. She had a joyful spirit and a good, strong voice. That would be important since, as Mrs. Murphy explained, Viola was going to be in disguise for most of the play. Everybody in Illyria was going to think that Viola was really Cesario, a young pageboy. Annie had to admit that Gabby's voice would be just right for the part. The hour was drawing to a close and Mrs. Murphy was hurrying to get through the first six character parts assigned. Just as the bell was about to ring, she announced, "And the part of Olivia will be read by Annie." Annie was stunned! She had not expected to be chosen for one of the major parts. Several people around her congratulated her and said that she would be a good choice for that part. The bell rang, and Annie stayed seated in her desk. She couldn't move. She looked at Mrs. Murphy, who grinned back at her.

"Um. Mrs. Murphy?" Annie stammered.

"Yes, Annie. You will do a fine job with her. Now, off you go. If you don't move, you'll be late to your next class, and we can't have that, can we? Come ready to read tomorrow. I think you're going to do a really good job with this for me. Have a great day."

Annie gathered her things and got to her feet. She looked hard at Mrs. Murphy, who was still grinning at her knowingly.

That night, she got home as quickly as she could and googled *Twelfth Night,* finding the Sparks Notes website, which had been helpful to her before. She went to the part where they did the in-depth character analysis for the major parts and looked at what they had to say about Olivia.

It seemed to be saying that Olivia was a young lady who had suffered some serious personal losses. In the past year, both her father and her brother had died, leaving her in charge of a substantial household. Her Uncle Toby, whom everyone called Sir Toby Belch, was certainly old enough to run the house, but he was a drunk. A "ne'er-do-well," they said, which seemed to be an old term for someone who just never grew up. Apparently, he was going to be a very important character too, sort of the one who whips up some trouble and causes some chaos. Annie grinned to herself, remembering that Mrs. Murphy had assigned that part to Dylan. But—back to Olivia. Olivia was in mourning for the loss of her father and her brother, but there was more to it than that. For the past year, the Duke Orsino had been courting her, and although she acknowledges him to be a good man, she feels nothing for him. So, she wants him to leave her alone, but she can't quite bring herself to be openly rude to him. Instead, she tells him that she has sworn off the company of all men, having decided to live like a nun. But this all changes when the young pageboy named Cesario—who is really Viola in disguise—shows up at her house to court her on behalf of the Duke. Suddenly, Olivia finds herself "smitten" with the young pageboy, and she struggles with this awkward infatuation.

Annie sat back in her chair and closed her eyes. She remembered that funny little smile on Mrs. Murphy's face at the end of the hour. She realized what was going on. Mrs. Murphy had chosen her to read the part of Olivia, a young woman who had suffered some profound personal losses and who would eventually come back to life— through the salvation of romantic love.

Annie understood that Mrs. Murphy was trying to teach her something way beyond the Shakespearean play. She did not think it could be that easy to come back to life, and she saw no romantic love interest on the horizon for herself. So, the idea wouldn't work anyhow.

Chapter 30

The next morning, when Annie walked into her English class, Mrs. Murphy had changed all the art work, just like she always did when they started a new piece of literature. Suddenly, there was a whole new set of faces staring out at Annie from the bulletin boards. She went up to the boards and studied the art, wondering which of the characters was supposedly Olivia, the part she was chosen to read. Suddenly, Olivia— the real one—came up and joined her at the bulletin boards.

"Hey, Annie," she said. "How cool that you got chosen for the part of Olivia! I would kind of like to read it because that's my name, but the truth is—I am really not a good reader, or public speaker. My eyes skip ahead and get the words all tangled up. Pure panic. But, maybe I will get a little part. I think I could handle that."

Mrs. Murphy came and joined them at the front of the room. "Good morning, girls," she said. "Are you ready to read Olivia for me today, Annie?"

Annie smiled at her nervously. "Don't you think you should maybe have chosen Olivia to read Olivia, Mrs. Murphy? Doesn't that make more sense?"

Olivia gasped in mock horror. She said, "No way! You chose right, Mrs. Murphy. I think if this play is going to come to life in this classroom, you are going to need good, strong voices to carry the parts. And Annie should be able to do a really good job with Olivia. But I will take a little part if you think I can handle it, when the time comes."

Mrs. Murphy smiled warmly, right at Olivia. "You know, you are pretty smart. You absolutely nailed it. If this play has any chance of coming to life, it will depend on the readers who are doing the big parts. But, I will tell you something, Olivia. There are two characters that I didn't get to assign yesterday because I ran out of time. And I was waiting for someone to tell me that they want to read. And you're the first person to do that! So, I'm going to ask you to read the part of Maria. Now, Maria is part of the downstairs crew in this play. She is the personal servant of Olivia, her lady-in-waiting. And she is also her best friend. Although Maria can be very proper, she can also be a little bit naughty. I sometimes get the feeling that she wishes that Olivia would let go of her mourning and allow herself to come back to life, so to speak."

While Mrs. Murphy was saying all of this, she was looking right at Olivia, not at Annie. But Annie could not help but feel that she was very aware that Annie was listening, and she meant for her to hear everything she was saying.

Olivia looked very carefully at Mrs. Murphy and nodded. She said, "I would be honored to read that part for you, Mrs. Murphy. And I would be honored to be the personal servant to this one here," she jerked her thumb at Annie playfully. Annie was again surprised at how clever Olivia really was. In subtle ways that a lot of people did not take time to notice.

Mrs. Murphy smiled and said, "Well done then. I will hear you both in your assigned parts today. Although we might not get to meet your character until tomorrow, Annie. Anyhow. Thanks, Olivia. You will be my Maria." She turned from them and walked over to her desk as the warning bell rang.

Having introduced the play in broad strokes yesterday, Mrs. Murphy was ready to dive right in today. And so was everyone in the class. There was a buzz and a hum in the classroom this morning, and just as the first hour of the day began, a light snow started to fall outside. It was one of those magical early December snows, with flakes as big as quarters, drifting softly down in the windless morning. Everyone stared out the windows, watching the magical transformation start to happen once again. It was old magic, that's for sure, but it was magic just the same.

Mrs. Murphy gathered their attention back into the classroom. "Good morning, everyone," she said. "I told you yesterday that this play has a very subtle winter subtext, or Christmas setting. And it is as if Mother Nature is helping me with my lecture, sending the first snowfall of the season to underscore what I am about to say. I will eventually explain why the title of this play is *Twelfth Night*, and if I forget to do so, you remind me. But, I want you to notice that the play also has a subtitle, called *What You Will.* You know what Shakespeare is suggesting by using that as a subtitle? He is very quietly saying this to you—this may not be how real life is, but wouldn't it be nice if it were? This is 'What you would like life to be like' or 'What you will.' Do you understand? So, right from the beginning, he is acknowledging that this little story may require a 'willing suspension of disbelief.' And you remember what that means, because I told you about that yesterday." She looked around the room. Every eye was on her. Annie felt her own excitement bubbling right underneath the surface. She had the feeling that this was going to be fun. Although reading out loud for everyone might also be terrifying.

Mrs. Murphy went on, "Now, the first scene begins with Duke Orsino bemoaning his alleged unrequited love. I say alleged because I am pretty sure that he is just sort of showing off, indulging in self-pity. Anyhow, it seems that he has been sending messengers to the Lady Olivia for almost a year now, and she has given him no encouragement. Jack—you have accepted the part of Duke Orsino. Now, be careful not to go too far, but understand that the truth is—he is more in love with the idea of being in love than he is in love with Olivia. He seems to want everyone to know that he is suffering. So, he puts on a show of being very sad. He has two friends in this scene who seem to be mocking him a little. Let's read the scene and see if we can pick up on these ideas. So, Jack, you begin for us."

Jack took the lead, and two other students pitched in and read the scene very smoothly. Annie sat there and listened and wondered when her part would show up. Now that it was really happening, she started to panic. She had been chosen for one of the most important parts in the play. Everyone was doing a really good job with the reading, and she started to wonder if she could hold up her end of the bargain.

The whole hour went by, and her character did not show up. But Olivia's did. She had to read the part of Maria for scene three, and it became clear that Maria was more than a little bit naughty. She even had a couple jokes or puns on words that were a little shocking. The part required that the person reading the lines have kind of a naughty twinkle in her voice, and surprisingly—Olivia did a great job with it!

In fact, at the end of the hour, several other students came up to Olivia and congratulated her on reading so well. Olivia blossomed in the glow of their praise, and Annie was so happy for her. It all made her even more nervous about her part, and when she peeked ahead, she saw that Olivia had a big scene the next day.

She decided that she would look at the part that night, just to have a heads-up on what she was going to have to say. As they were leaving at the end of the class, Mrs. Murphy grinned at Olivia and said, "Great job with Maria, Olivia. And Annie—be ready for Olivia tomorrow." She smiled at Annie, and Annie gulped.

The next day, the class started with Act I, scene 5. Mrs. Murphy explained that this was the scene where Viola, now in disguise as Cesario, goes to Olivia's house to try to win her heart for Duke Orsino. Except the problem is that Viola has secretly fallen in love with Orsino. The three days that they have spent together have melted her heart. She sees that Orsino is very handsome, and very confused about the nature of love. She is convinced that he only thinks he is in love with Olivia and that he really doesn't have a clue. Nonetheless, her feelings for him are all for naught because he seems to regard her almost as a kid brother. He thinks she is a pageboy, and nothing more. What a mess. And now, although she is crazy about Orsino herself, she has to try to win this lady's love for him. The cool thing about the way that Mrs. Murphy taught was that she gave the class a good description of what was going to happen in the scene before they read it out loud. And she had chosen good voices for each of the characters.

This scene was a long one, and it took her a while to get it all straight for them, but then they just dug in and read it. No questions were allowed during the reading, but all kinds of questions erupted during the session afterwards, where they analyzed the scene together and marked important passages. The thing about this scene was that it felt like this was where the bizarre love triangle really got started. And it was kind of funny. Orsino thinks he is in love with Olivia, who does not love him. Olivia is falling in love with the pageboy Cesario, who is really Viola. Viola is falling in love with Orsino, and he thinks she's a boy. What a disaster.

Toward the end of the scene, Gabriella was reading Viola, and Annie was reading the part of Olivia. And, it became clear, as the lines went on that poor Olivia was quite smitten with the pageboy, just like Mrs. Murphy said. She was rather openly flirting with the pageboy, who was really a girl. The lines went like this:

Viola: Lady, you are the cruelest she
alive. If you will lead these graces to the
grave. And leave the world no copy.

Olivia: O, sir, I will not be so hard-
hearted! I will give out diverse
schedules of my beauty. It shall be
inventoried and every particle labeled.

Viola: I see you what you are. You are
too proud. But if you were the devil,
you are fair. My lord and master loves
you. O, such love could be but
recompensed thou you were crowned.
The nonpareil of beauty.

Olivia: How does he love me?...What
would you do?

Furthermore, it became clear that Olivia was
asking the "pageboy" if he had any feelings
for her, or if he could see his way to being
attracted to her. Poor Olivia was making a
complete fool of herself, and the character
Viola could only feel pity for her. It seemed
to take Viola a while to even realize what
was going on. And when she did, she got out
of there as fast as she could. But Olivia
summoned her butler, Malvolio, and made
him chase the pageboy down, pretending
that he had left a ring with her that she did
not want. Annie could kind of feel sorry for
Olivia, because she was clearly making a

huge mistake, and she didn't even seem to care that she was making a fool of herself.

When they finished reading the scene, a couple people turned around and grinned at Annie, whispering to her that she had done a good job with the reading. Annie could feel herself blushing, but the truth is that it had been pretty easy to read against Gabriella, who had also done a really good job with the part.

Then, the fun began. Annie liked this part best—the part where they went over the lines and Mrs. Murphy pointed out what was important in the scene, and they got to ask questions. A girl named Lily, who was usually very soft-spoken, put her hand up and said, "Mrs. Murphy, I don't mean to be difficult, but I can see a problem here. If poor Olivia really falls in love with Cesario, who doesn't even exist, how in the world could there be any kind of a happy ending to the play?"

Mrs. Murphy smiled at her and said, "You have asked a very good question, Lily. And it is one that scholars, even today, are still debating. Now, we have a lot more of the play to read before we can answer that question, and even at the end of the play, you may have some misgivings. However, I will say two things right now. First. Remember that when you are reading a piece of literature, you are like a judge hearing testimony from a lot of different

255

witnesses. Wait until all the testimony is in before you render your judgment. Second. We may have to engage in that 'willing suspension of disbelief' that I told you about earlier. However, the way your mind is working—looking for the path to joy—is exactly the right mindset for dealing with a Shakespearean festive comedy. And now—the hour is upon us. We will finish our discussion of this scene and move on tomorrow. Thank you, readers. Well done."

The bell rang, and everyone started to shuffle out. It had been a fun hour, and it had flown by. A couple kids actually stopped by Annie's desk and told her that she did a good job reading the part of Olivia. She thanked each one of them, hardly believing her own ears. She stopped by Mrs. Murphy's desk to tell her that she had enjoyed doing the reading.

Mrs. Murphy grinned at her and said, "You did a really nice job with that part. I had a feeling that you would. And the whole class benefits from a good reading. It makes the play come to life, right in our classroom. And suddenly, it's not something that someone wrote 400 years ago. We breathe life right into it. So, it's an important job you've got. And finally, I think maybe—just maybe—the character of Olivia might have something to teach you." She smiled with such a gentleness that Annie felt her heart kind of tremble for a minute.

"What do you mean by that?" she asked softly.

"Wait and see," said Mrs. Murphy. "Let the play open up like a flower for you. And listen with your heart." Annie looked at her, stupefied. Mrs. Murphy said the most bewildering things sometimes. She had never had a teacher like this before.

She found herself looking forward to English class every day. And it seemed like everyone else did, too. They came in early every morning, looked at the artwork on the bulletin boards, figuring out who was who. And then they settled in to the readings. New characters kept showing up, and Mrs. Murphy assigned the parts smoothly. Everyone embraced their responsibilities and kept the action moving forward. There were two clowns, or fools, in the play— Feste and Fabian. They seemed to be good friends, and neither one of them seemed to be even the least bit stupid. They were good-natured and quick-witted fellows, and they enjoyed a good prank. Their favorite partner in jest was the drunken Sir Toby Belch, read very convincingly by Dylan. A couple times, Mrs. Murphy had to tell him to tone it down, as he was getting a little carried away with the drunken hiccupping. But he seemed to take the criticism in stride, and everyone knew that he was doing a great job with the part. And, like Mrs. Murphy had said, the play seemed to come to life right in their classroom. 400 years seemed to disappear, and the characters started to feel like someone you actually knew.

One day, at the beginning of the hour, Mrs. Murphy explained that there used to be a holiday in England called the Feast of Fools, and on that day, the naughtiest fellow in town was crowned king for a day. He was called the Lord of Misrule, and Sir Toby was a perfect example of what that person was like. He was trying to whip up as much drunken revelry and partying as he possibly could. This feast was held on the twelfth day after Christmas, and the evening of that feast was called Twelfth Night. When the "twelfth night" was over, it was time to return to your responsibilities—but hopefully, with a lighter heart.

Meanwhile, Viola's twin brother, Sebastian, arrives in Illyria. It had been three months since the shipwreck, and he believes that his twin sister, Viola, is dead. However, when Viola had created the character of Cesario, she had modelled him after Sebastian—imitating the way he dresses, talks, and walks. So, when Sebastian shows up in Illyria, everyone thinks he is Cesario, the pageboy to Orsino. He, of course, doesn't know what they are talking about.

Sebastian had come to town with a man named Antonio, a sea captain who had saved him from the shipwreck. Antonio and Orsino are enemies, so Antonio tells

Sebastian that he cannot be discovered in this town—he owes Orsino money which he cannot repay. So, Sebastian goes to town alone, and Antonio stays behind at the inn. Sebastian doesn't come home when he is expected, and Antonio goes out to find him. Instead, he finds Viola, disguised like a pageboy, being challenged to a duel by one of Sir Toby's buddies, and poor old Antonio thinks the person in trouble is Sebastian. Viola is really scared, and the whole thing is not the least bit funny to her.

So, when Antonio steps in to save her, poor Viola is very glad for his help. However, he is almost immediately arrested by Duke Orsino's men, who have been watching for him, having heard that he is in town. Meanwhile, Sebastian runs into Olivia, and she asks him to marry her, thinking she is speaking to the pageboy Cesario. But it's really Sebastian, who is completely bewildered, but very interested!

The confusion has reached the crisis moment, and it doesn't seem like any kind of a happy ending is possible. Several good people are in danger—real danger, and nobody knows what is really going on. The class finished the reading of Act 3, scene 4, and they were almost exhausted from the chaos of it. Annie could tell that a lot of people had a lot of questions. However, before the discussion of the scene really got going, Lily put her hand up, and Mrs. Murphy called on her.

Lily said, "I remember what you told me, Mrs. Murphy, and I've been waiting and watching. But I think I see the path to happiness now."

Mrs. Murphy said, "Good. Lead the way. Help us think it out, Lily."

"Well," said Lily. "Olivia has been falling in love with Cesario, who is really Viola. So, there is no way that works out for her. But here comes Sebastian, and he looks so much like Viola—except in male form—that maybe she could fall in love with him instead. And Viola is crazy about Orsino, and she's been trying to tell him that for three months, and he just doesn't listen. But he clearly values his time with her—I mean him. Or, maybe I really mean her. Anyhow. He has told us that he has shared all the secrets of his soul with Cesario. Maybe he could learn to love her instead of Olivia, whom he really doesn't love anyhow. He's just been playacting at that love. So—Viola would be happy, and Olivia would be happy, and Orsino might learn to be happy. As for Sebastian..."

"Great job, Lily," Mrs. Murphy said. "You've certainly taken us most of the way there. But there are some questions still to be answered. Can anyone make a list of problems we still have to solve?"

Nick put his hand up. He said, "I can think of several problems. First—will Sebastian fall in love with Olivia? Second—will Orsino forgive Viola for lying to him and pretending she's a guy? I mean, he told her a lot of things in confidence—guy to guy—and now he finds out that she is not a guy, but a girl that has a crush on him."

"Well done, Nick," said Mrs. Murphy. "Those are pretty substantial plot elements, and we will have to watch Shakespeare as he tries to convince us that all of this can work out. Well, you will notice, if you look at your books, that Act 4 is very short, and Act 5 is only one scene long. The bulk of the play is done, and Shakespeare just has to pull off these magic tricks at the end here. We should be able to do Act 4 tomorrow and Act 5 on Friday. And then, the magic of the Christmas holiday will be upon us. See you tomorrow, everybody, and once again—thank you to all the readers."

As she left the classroom, Annie swung by Mrs. Murphy's desk to say thank you again, and to let her know how much she was enjoying the play. Olivia was right beside her—the real Olivia—and she echoed Annie's sentiment. Olivia said, "But Mrs. Murphy. What is going to happen to my character Maria. It seems like Shakespeare has kind of forgotten about her."

261

"Not so, Olivia," said Mrs. Murphy. "You will see that Maria has her final scene tomorrow, and there is a happy ending in store for her too. An appropriately happy ending. And a little surprising. You will see what happens tomorrow. And Friday." She smiled at the two of them. "It's been fun, hasn't it? And you, Annie. I told you that Shakespeare's Olivia had something to teach you. Have you been trying to figure that out?"

"Yes, I have, Mrs. Murphy, and it's kind of sneaking up on me. I'm not ready to try to put it into words, but it's there, like a shadow in the back of my mind."

Mrs. Murphy smiled and said, "What a great description of an idea taking shape, Annie. Well, have a good day girls." The second hour class was already arriving, and Annie and Olivia got on their way to their own second hour classes.

After school, Annie went by her dad's room to see if he was ready to go home, or if she should walk. He told her that he had arranged for the little kids to have a ride home from one of the other moms, and he said he needed to stay for about an hour to work on a lab. He told Annie that she was welcome to stay and do her homework while he worked. But it wasn't very cold and there was a light snow, and Annie decided to walk home. She told her dad that she would meet him there, and she would make mac and cheese for dinner. He smiled and told her that would be great, and then he said, "Oh, Annie. I wanted to tell you. I invited Mrs. Murphy to come for dinner this Friday. It's the last day of school, and I thought it might be nice to start the vacation by having dinner together." He looked at Annie for approval. So much was unsaid in his look. Annie could tell that he was nervous, wanting to be careful about all of this.

Annie looked hard at him. "Are you guys sort of going out now?" she asked. "I mean—I understand if you are. It's been over two years since Mom died, and she would not want you to mourn for her forever. She would want you to live the rest of your life. So, I don't have a problem with it. I just kind of want to know what's really going on."

Her dad looked at her for a long time before speaking. Annie could see him gathering his thoughts, and trying to say things just the right way. "I didn't want to upset you, Annie. Because it's Christmas time, and your mom loved Christmas." He smiled sadly. "Maybe more than anyone I ever met—your mom loved Christmas. And I didn't want to ruin any of those memories. But, I really like Mrs. Murphy—her name is Jessica, by the way. And I would like your permission to say that we are going together, or whatever they call it these days. She's lonely and I'm lonely, and we make each other laugh. So, I would like your permission to date her a little bit and see if it fits at all." He looked suddenly like a bashful schoolboy.

Annie smiled, "Will it be awkward for you with both of you working here together at the high school?"

Her dad said, "We've thought about that. But it seems like a lot of people here actually think that we could be good for each other. And we are going to go very slowly. Not jump to any conclusions or anything."

Annie smiled, "Well, you have my permission to try it out. I really like her, Dad. She's become more than just a teacher to me. I don't exactly know how to describe what that is, but I know it's something more."

Her dad sighed a big sigh of relief. "She thinks the world of you, Annie. She says that she enjoys every minute of you being in her class. That you're really good at English. I guess you get that from your mom. She was a genius when it came to that kind of stuff."

"Anyhow," said Annie. "I think I'll walk home. It's just a light snow out there, and you remember what Charlie Brown always says."

Her dad smiled at her. "No, I'm sorry to say—I don't remember what Charlie Brown always says."

Annie grinned at him and said, "December snowflakes are the sweetest. See you at home."

Chapter 31

That night, Annie's dad surprised everyone by coming home with a beautiful Christmas tree. It was a real one, and it had ice and snow on it. He got it in the house and put it in the tree stand. While Annie made the mac and cheese for dinner, the whole house started to smell like Christmas. As she was cooking and setting the table, her dad went up in the attic and got the boxes of Christmas ornaments down. He opened the boxes and the little kids pawed through them, looking for their favorites. Her dad wouldn't let them hang any ornaments until the tree had a chance to drop a little. Besides, he always did the lights before they put on ornaments.

Nevertheless, the whole feeling in the house had changed, simply by bringing the Christmas tree in. Her dad set it up in the living room, right in front of the picture window, right where it had always gone, all of Annie's life. She was thinking about this as she finished setting the table and checking her heart to see if it was aching more than usual. She carefully logged in her feelings and realized, once again, how much she missed her mom. But it wasn't a raw, open wound. More—a quiet kind of missing. She was starting to realize that it would never go away, this quiet hurt, but that she could breathe again. And laugh again. It was like she finally realized that she was coming back to life. It hurt, but it was also good.

They ate supper, and then the little kids couldn't wait any longer. Her dad opened the boxes of lights and ornaments, and the mayhem began. Eddie and Sarah started hanging the ornaments, and Annie pitched right in. Lots of people went for all white lights these days, but her mom and dad had always preferred the little colored lights. Her dad said that the tree seemed merrier to him with all the colors.

As she helped to decorate the tree, Annie paused to consider some of the homemade ornaments that she found in the boxes. Some that she had made back in kindergarten were still in pretty good shape. Annie was amazed at her dad's patience as the little ones frantically placed their chosen ornaments on the tree. Stepping back, Annie realized that the bottom half of the tree was much more decorated than the top half.

She whispered this to her dad, not wanting to upset Eddie and Sarah. He smiled at her and whispered back, "I know. I always secretly redecorate and reposition things after they have gone to bed. You just never noticed before. Your mom and I have always done that." He sounded wistful.

Annie smiled, feeling his sadness touching her. She said softly, "If you like, I could help you after they've gone to bed."

Her dad smiled. He said, "That would be very nice. Also, there's something I wanted to give you when we have a moment's peace." Then, he told the kids to finish up hanging the last ornaments because it was time for bed. Annie looked at her wristwatch and was surprised to see that it was almost ten o'clock. Good thing there were only two days left of school. And really only one day and a half-day on Friday, so they were almost there. Before he took the kids up to bed, her dad turned all the lights out except for the beautiful Christmas tree. Then he gathered all three of them into his arms and hugged them. "Merry Almost Christmas, you guys. You have been very good this year, and I believe Santa has noticed that."

Eddie pulled back and looked at his father quizzically. Annie knew that he wanted to ask the big question, but couldn't quite bring himself to do it, half knowing the answer already. As for Sarah, she was still young enough to be oblivious, and wanted to make sure that Annie would help her write her letter to Santa this weekend. Annie promised that she would.

Her dad took the little guys up to bed, and Annie finished tidying up the empty ornament boxes, which her dad would store away until they needed to dismantle the Christmas tree. But, for now, it smelled beautiful, and the lights twinkling in the darkness worked their old magic on her heart. It made her miss her mom more than ever, but at least she could admit that to herself. That was something.

She was just about to go upstairs when her dad came downstairs and said, "Come help me adjust these ornaments a little bit. Our poor tree is a little bottom heavy." Annie helped him move some of the ornaments up higher on the tree, and then she sat beside him on the couch. Quietly, he reached over to a side table and then he gave her a little box, and a Christmas card. "It's from your mom," he said quietly.

Annie's breath caught in her chest, and her eyes filled with tears. Filled, but they did not fall. She looked into her dad's eyes and saw his sadness, his loneliness, and his hope. "Read the card first," he said. "You know how organized your mom was. She told me to do it just like this."

Annie opened the card, trying hard not to blink. It was a picture of a beautiful deer, standing alone in the snow. The deer was a doe, and she had her face turned toward the reader. In the distance was a broken-down fence, suggesting a setting not unlike the entrance to the railroad tracks, where Annie had seen the mama deer and her baby. The narrow gate. Almost in spite of herself, Annie breathed in deeply and sharply. She hadn't told her dad about that day. She hadn't told anyone. Her dad was watching her closely.

He said, "Try not to be frightened or sad, Annie. She loved you so much. And I feel pretty certain that she is watching us this very moment, and this was so important to her." He reached out his hand and took Annie's hand in his, squeezing it gently. Annie nodded in understanding, not quite trusting herself to speak.

She opened the card and read her mom's handwriting. Her dad asked her to read it out loud, so she did. Softly. It said: *My darling Annie. Merry Christmas. I'm sorry I can't be there to hold you in my arms, but let your dad hug you when you are done reading this, and know that hug is from me. I love you so very much, and I am so very proud of you. The moment that you came into our lives, everything changed. For the better. Every moment was more meaningful, and it has been our greatest joy to watch you grow up into the beautiful young woman you are today. Here is my ruby ring. I've been saving it for you. Please wear it on your right hand, and every time you pick up a pen to write anything, you will know that I am with you. Loving you always. And I will come again, my dear, though it were ten thousand mile. Love, Mom*

Annie finished reading and her dad handed her the ruby ring, the one her mom always wore on her right hand. He slipped it on her ring finger, and it sparkled in the lights from the Christmas tree. Annie looked up at her dad, helplessly, and then she broke. She sobbed uncontrollably, soaking his dress shirt—which he still had on from work—with her tears. He held her in his arms and rocked her, ever so gently, not saying a word, just letting her cry. Annie felt as if she had been holding herself together so tightly, for so long. Once she let go and started crying, she just couldn't seem to stop.

She tried to tell her dad that she didn't feel worthy of her mom's high praise. She knew she had made some mistakes, particularly about drinking that beer at that party, and what an embarrassment it could have been for her dad, and she didn't even know why she had done it. She was blubbering all this out against her dad's chest, and he just kept stroking her hair. He took her by the shoulders and leaned her back and looked into her eyes.

"Annie," he said, very calmly, "you made a mistake that night, and you have done your penance several times over. I know it won't happen again. That night was a perfect storm, and anyhow, I am pretty sure that you will make another mistake. Sooner or later. You're only human after all." He dried her tears with his fingers, pushing her hair back off her face. "But your mom and I are so very proud of you. One of the reasons she was finally able to let go

271

peacefully was that she believed in you. You gave her permission to go, and I mean that in the best way possible. She needed your blessing, and you—because you are such a good person—you gave it to her."

"Oh, Dad," Annie said softly. "I miss her so much." Still the tears flowed.

"I know you do. So do I—more than I can say. But you have been such a big help to me with the little ones. And you're doing a great job in all of your classes— particularly English, from what I hear," he added, with a twinkle in his eye.

"Really, dad? Or are you just saying that because you and Mrs. Murphy are sweet on each other?"

Her dad chuckled. "Sweet on each other! What a charming, old-fashioned way of saying it. Your mom always told me that you were an old soul." He smiled to himself. "No. I'm not just saying it. Mrs. Murphy has told me that you are one of the most naturally gifted students she has ever taught. As for what is between her and me—well, I guess you could say that we are sweet on each other. I honestly don't know if anything will become of it all, but it is nice to have a friend. And she is a good friend to me. I hope you can understand that."

"I do, Dad. I had a hard time in the beginning. I just couldn't get over the idea that in liking her, both you and I—but mostly you—were somehow being unfaithful to Mom. But I'm getting past that idea. I know this sounds crazy, but we are reading a play called *Twelfth Night* in English class, and oddly enough—in the most subtle and surprising way—it's helping me figure some stuff out."

"Well, isn't that interesting," her dad said, smiling. "You should tell Jessica that."

"Jessica?" Annie said.

"Yes. Although you should still call her Mrs. Murphy. Still, before Christmas vacation starts, you should let her know that this play has helped you figure some things out, as you say. I bet that would make her very happy. And now," he said, looking at his wrist watch, "you should go to bed. You still have two days of school. Or—at least one and a half." He smiled.

"I will, dad. Thank you for this beautiful ring. I'm just going to sit here by the tree for a few minutes, and then I'll go up to bed."

He kissed her on the cheek and headed into his room, leaving Annie with the Christmas tree twinkling in the darkness. She sat for a while, looking at the ruby ring on her finger, remembering her mom and all her sweetness. Remembering her song. My luv is like a red, red rose. And I will come again, my dear, though it were ten thousand miles. The words of the song, the memory of her mom's voice, the twinkling lights on the tree, the ruby ring glimmering on her

finger—all worked their magic, and she felt
a kind of gentle peace come over her.

Chapter 32

On Thursday, they read all of Act Four in English class. They were really short scenes and the hour flew by. Several important things happened. Sebastian and Olivia met each other, and she asked him to marry her! He thought she was really pretty, and he told her that he wished he was the man she thought he was. Silly Olivia thought he was playing word games with her and brushed his words away. It was a fun scene for Annie to read because Olivia was making a mistake, but it was a good mistake—one that would eventually lead her to happiness, or to joy.

Sir Toby, Feste, and Maria have a last laugh at Malvolio's expense. He is the pompous butler who is always trying to get everyone in trouble, so no one really feels very bad for him. And Feste—the most important fool—announces that things have gone far enough, maybe even too far. So, as Mrs. Murphy said to the class, they were all set up for the joyful conclusion, which they would read on Friday. But as the hour was ending, she said something very interesting.

She said, "Now, Shakespeare really knows what he's doing by the time he writes this play. He knows that some losses can never be undone, not in this life. For example, you remember at the beginning of the play that Olivia had lost her dad and her brother, both of them having passed away in the past year. Those losses cannot be undone. However, there are some losses that can be healed with the 'magic' that we find at the end of a comedy. Can anyone guess what some of those losses might be?"

Several hands went up quickly. A girl named Lia said, "Well, I think the first and most important loss that could be redeemed will be for Sebastian and Viola. Pretty soon, they are going to run into each other, and he's going to realize that his sister is still alive. And she will realize that her brother survived the shipwreck too! They haven't seen each other in three months, so that will be a joyful reunion."

"Very good, Lia," said Mrs. Murphy. "That is certainly the most important one. Does anyone else have any other ideas about the kind of healing that might be about to take place? Maybe not that dramatic, but important nonetheless."

Brendon said, "I think that Olivia will realize that she can marry Sebastian instead of Cesario. Because Cesario doesn't even really exist. And Sebastian seems like a really good guy."

Gabriella said, "I see what you're saying, but should we be happy about that? I mean, if she's really in love with Viola, should we be happy that she will settle for marrying Sebastian? Is that a safe substitution? I'm not really sure that you ought to accept a substitute when it comes to love. It's too important."

Mrs. Murphy chuckled and said, "Well, let's see. I don't think there is anything safe about falling in love. But you have asked a very good question, and it is one that scholars are still debating in our time. Still, I think we can fall back on our idea of a 'willing suspension of disbelief' in this case, at least to some extent." She looked around the room, aware that the bell was about to ring. "Any other ideas?"

A girl named Stacy, who sat way in the back next to Dylan, raised her hand. "I hope that Orsino sees that Viola loves him, and that he is ready to love her. But I can see that as being potentially very awkward." She giggled as she said this.

"Well done, Stacy," Mrs. Murphy said. "You have hit the nail on the head. It will be a dangerous moment, and yet, it has to work out for us to be happy for Viola, right? Any other ideas?"

Dylan put his hand up and said, "What about me? I mean, what about Sir Toby?" Just as he was speaking, the bell rang and everyone got to their feet. Mrs. Murphy smiled and said that tomorrow's scene would answer all these questions. Annie realized that Mrs. Murphy had timed things so that the last scene would be read on the last day before Christmas vacation. She was starting to realize that Mrs. Murphy seemed to be blessed with perfect timing, but she suspected that although it looked like a happy accident, it was really very well planned.

It had been such a fun hour that Annie didn't want to leave and go to her next class. She wanted to tell her about what she had realized last night, but there were too many other kids around for something as serious as that. However, she remembered that her dad had told her that she should let her know, and she made herself a promise that she would do it tomorrow.

Finally, it was Friday. The last day before Christmas vacation. She and her dad helped the little kids wrap up Christmas presents for their teachers, and Sarah had to bring in two dozen Christmas cookies. So, the morning was a panic, getting everything in place. But they managed to get them to school on time and get to their homerooms.

As soon as homeroom was over, it was time to begin English class. The last day of *Twelfth Night*. Annie would be sad to see it end. Everyone in the class seemed to feel the same way. Several kids dropped little Christmas gifts on Mrs. Murphy's desk. Annie had made brownies last night, and she had put six of them in a Christmas tin and tied a red ribbon around the tin. She had also written a short note, trying to express her thanks for what Mrs. Murphy had gently given her. She had written: "Dear Mrs.

Murphy—thank you for being such a good friend to my Dad, and to me. Thank you for giving me permission to rejoin the dance. Your student, Annie."

She had written the note right before she went to bed, and she wasn't really sure if it worked. She was trying to use a metaphor for a pretty complicated idea. It was building off something that Mrs. Murphy had said way back when she introduced the play— that all of Shakespeare's comedies had the theme of "Carpe diem." And that some of the characters embrace that idea, and some of them are just determined to be miserable. Annie knew that Malvolio was going to be the one to fall into that category. He just had never learned to laugh at himself, and he had no desire of learning that now. She realized that all four of the young lovers—Olivia, Viola, Sebastian, and Orsino—were going to have to swallow their pride, to a certain extent, and take a chance on love and life. They were going to join the dance again, and so—with that idea in mind—she had written her note, hoping that Mrs. Murphy would get it.

All the students took their seats, and, once again—as if by magic—it started to snow outside. The sky grew dark and wintry, and it really felt like Christmas time to Annie. She could feel the excitement in the classroom; everyone wanted to hear the happy ending that they felt pretty sure was coming. After the bell rang, Mrs. Murphy got them ready to do the last scene together. As always, Annie knew that she would tell them what would happen in the final scene, and then they would read it. Annie thought this was very helpful, because you had a better chance of reading the lines with some understanding of what you were saying. Since she was reading the part of Olivia, she always paid very careful attention to what Mrs. Murphy said she was feeling and thinking. Annie had realized that she had a sort of obligation to do the part as well as she could. Everyone in the class was counting on her—or at least, that's what it felt like.

"Good morning, everyone," said Mrs. Murphy. "Thank you for all of your kind notes and gifts. I hope that each and every one of you has a very merry Christmas vacation. And that you are with people you love. Now, let's do this final scene, so you can see how Shakespeare pulls this all together." All the students opened their books to act five, eager to hear how it all works out.

Mrs. Murphy said, "The scene opens with the last echoes of confusion. Orsino has apparently heard that the Lady Olivia has been flirting with his pageboy Cesario, and he is angry and embarrassed. He has Viola in tow, and he has come to Olivia's house to see if this is really true. Several times, Viola tries to explain that she meant no harm, but he hushes her. Feste tries to get some money out of Orsino with some of his clever word games. Orsino is not in the mood for his witty banter and sends him to get Olivia. Antonio is brought before Orsino, and, seeing Viola, thinks he is seeing Sebastian. He feels hurt that Sebastian has betrayed him. Viola is bewildered. Olivia comes on stage and tells Orsino that she has just married his pageboy, and Viola sputters in indignation. Finally, the real Sebastian comes on stage—dressed just like Viola—and everybody stops dead, staring at them. Stupefied! Are they seeing double?" Annie found herself trying to picture all of this confusion.

Mrs. Murphy went on, "Finally, Sebastian and Viola figure out what is really going on, and they are overjoyed. Then, of course, each of them turns to the person that they have fallen in love with—Sebastian to Olivia and Viola to Orsino—to see how they will handle this revelation. I don't want to steal the thunder of the scene, so I will let you see them work it out, and then we will talk. That leaves us with several questions to answer, mainly concerning Toby and Maria, and, of course, Malvolio. Let's hear the lines, and then we will see what Shakespeare is telling us."

Everyone got settled and the scene began. Annie was careful to do Olivia's lines as clearly and confidently as she could. When it was all done, there were lots of questions.

"What about Sir Toby," Dylan asked. That had been his character. "He was such a big deal, and he really hardly even matters in the final scene."

Mrs. Murphy said, "You're exactly right. He only has a couple lines, and his presence doesn't seem to contribute much to the final scene. And it is startling, because he was so important to the play, particularly in the middle scenes. But we do find out something very important. We find out that he has married Maria, and if ever there was someone who could handle Sir Toby, and maybe even make him happy—she's the woman. And so, we could say that Sir Toby and Maria join the dance of life." When she said that, Annie's heart skipped a beat. She looked up at Mrs. Murphy to see if she had said that on purpose. And she saw her smile, just a little smile, right at her. But she kept right on teaching.

A girl named Emily, who sat in the front row, said, "I'm interested in Feste's last song. The closing song. What does it mean? The rain it raineth every day."

Mrs. Murphy smiled at Emily and said, "What do you think it might mean? I'll grant you—it's an unusual closing for the play. Not completely joyful, right?"

Emily said, "I wonder if Shakespeare is too smart to be completely joyful. If he is trying to remind us that when moments of happiness come, we ought to enjoy them, because the rain—or sorrow—will inevitably return. The rain it raineth every day."

Mrs. Murphy smiled at Emily, "Honestly, Emily. I don't think I could have said it any better myself." Then she turned her attention on the whole class. "So, what do you think about Malvolio. The prank against him is found out, and the perpetrators are not punished. As Fabian says, it does not seem a time for punishment, but rather for joy. So, the big question is— how do you feel about that? Do you feel sorry for Malvolio or not?"

A pretty girl named Paige said, "I feel sorry for him. He thought that Olivia was in love with him, and now he finds out that the others were just playing a trick on him, and she was not attracted to him at all. Seems like a classic case of bullying to me. And he storms out there, trying to save his last shred of dignity. Poor guy."

Nick put up his hand, "I understand what you're saying, Paige. And that's very nice. But, I find myself not feeling sorry for him at all. He wasn't really in love with Oliva so much as he was in love with the idea of being a rich man. All her gold and jewels. And he is always mean to everyone, lording it over them and trying to get them all in trouble. I think they took him down a peg or two, but they didn't really hurt him. However, I think it would be hard for him to keep working there, after they have made such a fool of him."

Mrs. Murphy nodded and smiled. "I'm so impressed with how well all of you have learned to think and analyze and support your opinions with arguments from the text. You two have rather elegantly summed up the big debate about the end of this play. Many scholars are making a big deal about the treatment of Malvolio these days. So, you're right on the cutting edge with your analysis. Both of you. Now, the hour is upon us, so once again—have a wonderful winter break, and I will see you all next year! I always love saying that," she giggled as she announced this. Just then, the bell rang, and she added, "Oh, I forgot to say—no homework over break!" This last announcement was met with cheers, and everyone started filing out, wishing each other a Merry Christmas and Happy Holidays.

At the risk of being late to her next class, Annie stopped by Mrs. Murphy's desk. Mrs. Murphy said, "I got your card, Annie. And—you understood me perfectly. And I think you understood Shakespeare and Olivia too." She reached out for Annie and hugged her. Annie felt a quiet sense of joy.

She felt like, in that moment, Mrs. Murphy understood her perfectly, and she was very grateful. She felt a tear trickle down her cheek and reached up to dry it quickly. She stepped back from Mrs. Murphy and saw her smiling at her.

"Thank you, Mrs. Murphy. I hope you have a Merry Christmas, and I hope you get a chance to relax. Maybe go see a funny movie with some nice guy." She smiled, and Mrs. Murphy smiled right back.

"Maybe I will. Merry Christmas, Annie."

Chapter 33

After school, Annie went home and tried to
realize that she had no school for the next
two weeks. And really, no homework either.
All of her teachers had been very merciful.
Her dad came in, having picked up the little
kids after school, and she went outside in the
yard and helped them build a snowman. The
snow kept falling, and it really looked like
Christmas. Her dad ordered pizzas for
dinner, and the night was just perfect. After
dinner, they all sat in the family room and
watched *Home Alone*, Annie's favorite
Christmas movie. No matter how many
times she had seen it, it always made her
laugh. And she loved the way it helps us
realize that family is what matters.

The whole house smelled wonderful
because of the Christmas tree, and it just
seemed like a perfect night. She kissed her
dad goodnight and thanked him again for
her beautiful ring. He kissed her on the top
of her head and told her how proud he was
of her. She wondered what exactly he was
referring to, but she decided to leave the
moment alone. Her heart felt too full for
words, anyhow.

The next morning, she woke up to
brilliant winter sunshine. The world lay
under a blanket of white, but there was no
wind, and it seemed like she might be able
to get a run in. Her dad was in the kitchen,

reading the paper and drinking his coffee. She told him that she was going for a short run. He cautioned her to be careful about her footing in the snow.

Someone had been out to clear the roads, but not the sidewalks, so Annie started a nice, careful jog in the streets. She didn't want to fall or tweak her knee or her ankle, now that she was finally feeling whole again. It would be Christmas in two days now, and she had to finish her shopping for her dad and for the little kids. Maybe she could get her dad to take her to the mall this afternoon. Or maybe Olivia could get Pierre to drive them. Olivia.

She smiled, thinking about Olivia, who was in many ways kind of proper, reading the part of Maria for *Twelfth Night*. She had done a really good job with it. And then, Annie remembered that, at the end of the play, Maria was supposed to marry Sir Toby Belch. That would mean that Olivia (the real Olivia—her Olivia) would marry Dylan! No way. She smiled to herself, thinking of that unlikely combination.

She realized that Mrs. Murphy had chosen the parts very carefully, not only using good voices, but using something else too. She had chosen Annie to read Olivia, and Annie thought about that. The character Olivia had lost her brother and her father. And Annie herself had lost her mom.

Like the Olivia of *Twelfth Night*, Annie had suffered some real losses that could not be redeemed. Not in this life. But Olivia had found Sebastian by the end of the play, and she had recovered a sense of joy and wonder. She was able to go on living her life with a lighter heart. That is probably what Mrs. Murphy was saying, in her own little way.

But it was harder to figure out why Dylan was Sir Toby. Or maybe not. Sir Toby was a bad boy, always looking for a prank or a joke. And he drank too much. But, by the end of the play, he was going to marry Maria. And she was one tough chick. Maybe he just wanted to be loved, and maybe she could make him happy. Make him shape up. As for why Olivia (her friend) read the part of Maria? That was tough. Maybe it was to get Olivia to be a little bit naughty. Which she did very well, oddly enough. Anyhow, it sure had been fun, and Annie felt the gentle lessons of the play still resonating in her heart.

Everybody suffers the loss of a loved one. In time. It is part of the human condition. You have to mourn that loss, and the truth is—you will never be the same. But you honor that person, and your love for them, by living your life to the fullest.

You should embrace the chance for love when it comes along, for the rain it raineth every day. You should try to be honest and caring, and do the right thing. That is what Viola did, and things worked out for her. No guarantees, of course. But still.

Annie looked around and realized that she was at the narrow gate—the entrance to the trail she had run with the cross-country team. The trail where she had seen the mommy deer and her baby last fall. She realized that she was actually hot. Since there was little to no wind, the sun had warmed her thoroughly.

She found a nice, dry rock right by the entrance to the trail. She looked for the wild rose that had bloomed there last fall, but she could not find any blossoms. The vine was there, but it had lost all of its leaves. It was asleep for the long winter now. She sat down right by the narrow gate.

She thought about what she had figured out that day—that the narrow gate could be a metaphor for loss, or pain, or sorrow. That everyone eventually had to pass through it, but that on the other side, there might be a quiet kind of joy. A deeper joy. A Christmas joy. If that made any sense. She took off her hat and closed her eyes. There was almost no sound at all. Tiny little sounds, of branches hitting each other very lightly in the breeze. Of birdsong. She let her mind drift and soon she was asleep. Sitting on the rock in the sun. By the old trail.

Suddenly, there was a sound. The sound of someone singing, not very well. Puzzled, she opened her eyes to see Dylan, sitting right beside her. She listened for minute, trying to figure out what he was singing.

> O mistress mine, where are you roaming?
> O stay and hear! Your truelove's coming,
> That can sing both high and low.
> Trip no further, pretty sweeting,
> Journeys end in lovers meeting,
> Every wise man's son doth know.

His musical pitch was terrible. Annie kind of recognized the tune he was using under the words. She thought it might be "God Rest Ye Merry Gentlemen." Sort of. Badly mangled, but still—it was there.

She looked at him in complete astonishment. But he did not stop singing until he got to the last line. Then, she clapped her hands, applauding his effort. He was laughing. She was laughing too.

"Did you like that? Was I good?" he asked, grinning.

"No!" Annie gasped. "You were absolutely terrible! But also, wonderful, at the same time, if that makes any sense. But what are you singing that for? That's Feste's song—the wise and witty clown. And you were not Feste—you were naughty Sir Toby."

"I know," he grinned. "And at the time I got that part assigned to me, I thought it was perfect. It was the part I really wanted. But as the play went on, I wished I had Feste instead. The wise and witty fool, as you say. I liked him better." He stood up and grabbed her hand, standing her up too. "You did a great job with Olivia, by the way. I didn't know you were such a good actress."

Annie stood and brushed the snow off her butt. "Well, it's not acting, exactly. Just reading out loud. But I really did enjoy it. I'm going to miss that play, but I'm looking forward to next semester. I wonder what she will teach us next." Annie realized that she felt a profound sense of trust for Mrs. Murphy, and a willingness to be guided by her. To learn more—about literature, and about life.

They started walking back out to the street. "I'll walk you part of the way home," Dylan said. "If that's all right with you?" She nodded that it would be fine. "Then, I really have to go Christmas shopping. I haven't bought my family presents yet. But I agree with you. I really enjoyed reading that play. What lesson did you learn from *Twelfth Night*?" Dylan asked.

"Mostly to take the opportunities for joy when they come along," Annie answered.

Dylan stopped walking and pulled her close. "I was thinking the same thing myself." He kissed her on the cheek. Her eyes grew wide. That was the first time she had been kissed by a boy and it actually meant something. What it meant, she wasn't exactly sure yet. But she felt a sense of joy again. A sense of happiness. She thought about her mom and her dad and the little kids. And Christmas coming. And this handsome boy standing in front of her who had just kissed her on the cheek. And she smiled softly and rejoined the dance.

Made in the USA
Lexington, KY
02 September 2019